**The Republic of Consciousness Prize 2021
(Shortlisted)**

'Summons the ghosts of Sebald and Borges but with a poise
and originality that is all Sagasti's own.
John Mitchinson

'A bewitching suite of stories about music, heard and
unheard.'
Boyd Tonkin, *The Arts Desk*

'A beautiful, fragmentary rendition which never strikes a
false note.'
The Irish Times

'Sagasti's careful contrapuntal construction weaves together
an eclectic range of vignettes which transcend their
parts, leaving an indelible emotional impact that defies
rationalisation.'
Gutter

'A veritable fugue of insights and literary forms, subtlety and
humour.'
Asymptote

A MUSICAL OFFERING

First published by Charco Press 2020
Charco Press Ltd., Office 59, 44-46 Morningside Road, Edinburgh EH10 4BF

Work published with funding from the 'Sur' Translation Support Programme of the Ministry of Foreign Affairs of Argentina / Obra editada en el marco del Programa 'Sur' de Apoyo a las Traducciones del Ministerio de Relaciones Exteriores y Culto de la República Argentina.

A CIP catalogue record for this book is available from the British Library.

ISBN: 978-1-9993684-5-6
e-book: 978-1-9162778-1-6

www.charcopress.com

Edited by Robin Myers
Cover designed by Pablo Font
Typeset by Laura Jones
Proofread by Fiona Mackintosh

2 4 6 8 10 9 7 5 3

Luis Sagasti

A MUSICAL OFFERING

Translated by
Fionn Petch

CHARCO PRESS

CONTENTS

Lullaby 1

Silences... 31

The Great Organ of Himmelheim 59

Wars 65

Sky Ants 81

Exotic Birds.. 87

Da Capo 109

For Adriana

Now, I've heard there was a secret chord
That David played, and it pleased the Lord
But you don't really care for music, do you?

LEONARD COHEN, *Hallelujah*

The sound, cautious and muffled,
Of a fruit, fallen from the tree,
Amidst the unceasing melody
Of the deep forest quiet

OSIP MANDELSTAM
(Trans. A. S. Kline)

LULLABY

No one knows why an eighteenth-century Count, with no problems other than those that come with his position – palace intrigues, a damsel's jealousy, the tedium of protocol – is unable to make peace with his conscience and get to sleep at night, as is God's will and his own fervent desire. Like all of us, Count Keyserling believes that lying awake in the dark when everyone else has left for the land of Nod is a form of punishment. A punishment that equalises: insomnia makes no distinctions when it comes to expiating sins. As the nobility have always done, Count Keyserling attacks the symptom rather than the cause: he commissions the cantor of St. Thomas of Leipzig, one Johann Sebastian Bach, to create a composition that will lull him to sleep at last. In recompense he offers a silver goblet overflowing with gold louis. There was no need for such generosity; after all, it was the Count himself who had secured the composer his post in the Court of Saxony. Bach more than rises to the occasion, composing an aria to which he adds thirty separate variations. The compositions are linked not by the melody but by the bass line, the harmonic foundation.

The person charged with delivering these musical sleeping pills is an extraordinary harpsichordist who not only is capable of playing anything that is put in front of him but can also read a score upside down, like a rock star playing a guitar behind his back. His name is Johann Gottlieb Goldberg. He is young, which is to say impetuous and pretentious. Nevertheless, he practises the most difficult passages in the evenings, to avoid surprises. And he tries to find the right tempo that will help the nobleman drift off.

In honour of its first performer, and thanks to the alacrity with which he undertook his charge, posterity would christen this series of compositions the *Goldberg Variations*.

The most famous performance of the *Variations*, a feat not unlike swimming the Strait of Magellan, is by the Canadian pianist Glenn Gould. In fact, he recorded two: between them stretch twenty-six years in the life of a planet. The first version is as urgent and flamboyant as Baroque music permits, and was taped in 1955, when Gould was just twenty-three years old. The second is a recording made shortly before he died from a stroke at the age of fifty, in 1981. For all his genius, Gould couldn't escape the fate of the wise: the slower pace of the later version is that of someone who knows we only leave a circle before taking the first step.

Despite his surname, the Count is Russian, and an ambassador to the Court of Saxony. This makes for a reassuring diplomatic immunity, soirées (or rather, the palace lives in a permanent state of soirée), wild boar and candied treats in the evenings – and insomnia. Keyserling has a valet, who is more like a confidant. His name is Vasya and he only speaks Russian. Through the open door of the bedchamber, the music drifts in along with the draught – and sleep too, it is hoped. Vasya's task is to shut the door once he hears the Count snoring.

Spokoynoy nochi, he says just after ten. *Good night.*

The valet leaves the bedchamber, taking with him the candelabrum, which he carries to the adjacent room where Goldberg is waiting. He places it on a table and nods to indicate that the recital should begin.

Keyserling opens his eyes, observes the half-darkness of the room where the music comes from, and closes them again. The bedcovers are pulled up to his chin and he wears a nightcap.

Vasya, standing to one side, follows Goldberg's hands; Goldberg, the score.

The next day, the Count makes an observation, almost an order. The lapse between each variation should be shorter: when this gap of silence occurs, it is filled with expectation, making it impossible for him to fall asleep. On that first night, however, Vasya hears the Count snoring before the seventh variation begins. He closes the door to the room; Goldberg, the lid of the harpsichord. Where the corridor forks, they bid each other good night in Russian and in German. The valet descends the staircase. Goldberg heads for the other wing of the house in search of wine and conversation.

The pauses between each variation are no small matter – no pause is – and Glenn Gould knows this better than anyone. He has understood, and perhaps as the nights go by Goldberg perceives it too, that in reality there is no interruption between the movements: herein dwells the music that can only be found by the sense of touch. When Gould ends each of the variations, his body keeps moving, as videos clearly show; his left hand trembles blindly and his arm shifts: a dragonfly sensing the still-nascent music. He plays without a score.

In this interstice, in this crevasse that separates each variation, emerges the music that sends the Count to sleep. We may deduce that Gould is repeating Keyserling's own movements as he drifts into slumber. These slight spasms that occur during the pauses are known as myoclonic seizures. They are a contraction and relaxation of the muscle that we experience during the initial phases of sleep.

Practising, Goldberg discovers that the pauses between the variations shouldn't be uniform: for example, between the thirteenth and fourteenth, barely a breath should be taken, while between the seventh and eighth a more ample silence is imposed. That's not how he plays them, however: the idea is for the Count to get to sleep as quickly as possible, so the pauses must be short; Keyserling was clear about that (and he's the one paying, after all). On the second night the Count fails to recognise the melody; he has an ear for music and good taste, people say, but lacks a memory prodigious enough to notice if the music is the same, as he will only realise much later. This time, the first snores arrive during the eighth variation.

After the thirtieth variation, the work concludes with a *da capo* aria that introduces the idea of circularity. The first theme, which opens the series, is repeated at the end. Everything starts over.

This is Bach's surety, in the event that Keyserling fails to fall asleep.

And if sleep doesn't come, will the Count realise that everything has begun again? Will the same images illuminate his thoughts? Will his movements in bed repeat themselves?

There is a more or less widely held view that music and sleep share certain convolutions. In truth, they inhabit the present moment in very different ways. Music promises the pleasure of the future: anticipating a melody that flutters a few steps ahead is the dessert we savour even as we raise another steaming forkful to our lips. The present of sleep is pure mother's milk; there is nothing beyond it.

Should we see Goldberg as a reflection of Scheherazade? Each night, she staves off death with an unfinished story. This is no mean feat: to leave the Caliph with his mouth watering yet his stomach sated at the same time. Goldberg, on the other side of the looking glass, tells the same stories time and again, delivering the Count his little death every night.

One night, Scheherazade tells her own story: that of the woman who postpones her death with a new tale every night. It isn't the 602nd Night, which Borges makes so much of, although the translation of that Night by Cansinos Assens does include a detail that may have inspired him:

'Oh king! Here is a little bird that I have caught and that I bring to you, for it has such a beautiful voice! Because it trills in such a pleasant way!'
'Yes! Hurry to place it in a cage and hang it in my daughter's room, alongside her bed, so that it may distract her with its songs and its trilling...'

In an article for the review *Variaciones Borges*, the critic Evelyn Fishburn claims that the Night in question is the last of the stories to appear in the compilation made for the 1825 Breslau edition, which the translator Sir Richard Burton then added to the seventh and final of the supplementary volumes of a unique edition, known as the Luristan edition. This is where the framing story appears. Unlikely though it may seem, Borges must have had access to this rare edition. It's worth recalling his tale 'Tlön, Uqbar, Orbis Tertius...' In the story, the entry for *Uqbar*, which introduces the mystery, is only found in the last four pages of an 'inadequate' reprint of the *Encyclopaedia Britannica*.

Borges is the third director of the National Library to go blind. Two represent a coincidence; three, a confirmation, he writes, explaining his fate.

Quixote reads *Don Quixote*; Hamlet attends *Hamlet*, he always said.

The 602nd Night is the third blind man.

The threshold moon is the one shining the night before the thousandth sleepless night.

The threshold moon once more, among the stars that stream from Scheherazade's throat when she narrates her own story.

The next one, therefore, should be the same as the first in the series.

And everything should start over again.

Tracing a circle, standing in the centre and leaving death outside: that's the idea.

And if the Caliph recognises the stories? I mean, if he gets wise to the ruse? Might he already be so in love that he no longer cares if he's hearing the same song over and over?

Why risk it, Scheherazade.

The night when the circle begins to repeat itself is the open door she leaves in case death should appear at the end of a story. What they call an ace up the sleeve.

The following night, a new story.

But have we not heard this in countless songs that begin all over again after a refrain? Or when the volume gradually fades, giving the impression that the band is disappearing into the distance and the song is actually endless?

Staying on the moon, like children still unborn, the space between two lives that in Tibet they call *bardo* – isn't this the silence between the songs on an album, the distance between two movements of a symphony when it is heard for the first time?

(Nowadays this silence can only be found in the theatre; it's disappeared from our most private spaces – or does anyone actually still listen to an album right the way through?)

When I was little my mother would sing me the nursery rhyme 'Rock-A-Bye Baby', and when she got to the line 'down will come cradle, baby and all', the phrase 'baby and all' had a kind of lulling effect, a pleasant hum. *Babyandall, babyandall*, she went, to the rocking of the hammock. The fear only surfaced when the sounds took on meaning.

One night the Caliph, intrigued, asks a question: Where did you learn so many stories?

Scheherazade lowers her gaze. A different kind of silence emerges between them.

She says she heard them as a child from the mouth of her father, and from the mouth of her father's father.

She says she made them up, with Allah's blessing.

She says: from a dervish.

She says: from a canvas on which all the stories are embroidered, from a marvellous carpet that looks like the moon.

She says: in fact, if he were to listen very closely, she is always telling the same story.

And now, from the place that is *always*, a tanpura appears. A tanpura is an Indian stringed instrument with a large sound box that emits a constant hum of tense repose.

This is the sound we hear at the start of 'Tomorrow Never Knows', the John Lennon song inspired by the *Tibetan Book of the Dead*. Composed on a single chord, C, it has no chorus and is more like a mantra. The rest of the Beatles were actively involved in its creation. Paul brought with him a series of loops, tiny recordings no longer than four beats to be repeated endlessly, re-recorded faster or slower until their source can no longer be identified: it's thought that McCartney's own voice, a distorted guitar and clinking glasses transmigrated to become the seagulls that follow the tanpura.

And George Harrison recorded his guitar part backwards.

It begins with *Turn off your mind* and ends with *Play the game 'existence' to the end / Of the beginning.*

The meaning of the last line isn't very clear.

How do we know when the beginning reaches its end?

Where's the centre of the circle, Scheherazade?

For the sixteenth variation, the exact centre of the

Goldberg Variations, Bach composed an overture, that is, a new beginning.

'Tomorrow Never Knows' is the last song on the album *Revolver*. The next one, *Sgt. Pepper's*, is the first album in history without pauses between the songs, as if it were all one long composition.

The next song begins. There's no record of our stay on the moon.

I'm listening to the radio now and realise that no song is ever allowed to end: another one begins right away and another one after that, interrupted every now and then by some dumb Scheherazade saying how nice what we just heard is (yes, *nice*). An Islamic sleeplessness delivered by FM. Not even a crescent moon left for us to disappear into.

There is a radio frequency not far from Moscow that broadcasts a fleeting buzzing sound twenty-five times a minute. It has been playing for twenty-three hours and ten minutes every day for forty years now. The buzzing isn't generated internally but transmitted by a micro-phone. Sometimes, distant conversation can be heard. On 2 September, 2010, a snatch of *Swan Lake* came through: the 'Dance of the Cygnets'. Everything points to some military purpose behind all this, or some artful espio-nage-related deception. The transmission mast is located to the north of Moscow, on a hill in the middle of a forest. A male voice spoke the words 'Mikhail Dmitri Zhenya Boris' a month earlier. After these events, it seems the radio station changed position.

I doubt that the fragment of Tchaikovsky was a secret message for the spies. Someone played it when no one was meant to be listening. Yet someone was, and now it's on the internet.

What was this person doing, the one who heard *Swan Lake*?

Andy Dufresne, sentenced to life in prison for a crime he naturally didn't commit, locks himself in a jail administration office and plays an aria from *The Marriage of Figaro* over the PA. Just a minute's worth. On the other side of the door, the prison warden and the guards are yelling orders. He ignores them. As long as the music lasts, there's not a prisoner who doesn't look upwards, at the loudspeakers, at the sky. This is a scene from *The Shawshank Redemption*, based on the novella by Stephen King. 'I have no idea to this day what those two Italian ladies were singing about – Truth is, I don't wanna know. Some things are best left unsaid. I like to think they were singing about something so beautiful it can't be expressed in words. It makes your heart ache because of it. I tell you, those voices soared, higher and farther than anybody in a grey place dares to dream. It was like some beautiful bird flapped into our drab little cage and made those walls dissolve away. And for the briefest of moments, every last man at Shawshank felt free. Andy got two weeks in the hole for that little stunt.'

Led below decks by the captain of the boat carrying an opera singer's ashes to be scattered into the Aegean Sea, a group of illustrious guests – baritones and tenors among them – comes to the boiler room. From above, leaning against the handrail, they contemplate with shocked indulgence the sweaty, soot-faced boilermen.

It's not hard to see the captain as Virgil and the guests as Dantes. When they notice their distinguished visitors, the workers drop their shovels, clutch their caps to their chests, and beg them to sing. The monotonous martial roar of the engines forms a magnificent backdrop for the competing voices in C as they rise from the virile chests of the tenors, and for the glass-shattering trills of the sopranos. It's a close-up of heaven for the crew, while it's hell in someone else's voice for the divos, who close the scene with *La donna è mobile*, baring their teeth.

Fellini filmed this scene for his movie *And the Ship Sails On*.

No baby could fall asleep to 'Tomorrow Never Knows'.

The *Tibetan Book of the Dead*'s real title, *Bardo thodol*, means something like 'Liberation through Hearing'.

When a child first learns to hum a melody, the child stops being music and instead becomes a receptacle for remembering it.

Like the Beatles, Glenn Gould has made the recording studio a musical instrument in its own right. The final version of the *Variations* didn't emerge from a single session; in fact, the pianist selected the best cuts from several.

So what would it mean to listen to them all one after the other, without intervals? To hear what can only be played by artificial means.

The Beatles and Glenn Gould stop performing a year apart.

Where does a story end? Taking a classical viewpoint: is it when the knot has finally been untied? Though if we think about it, when a knot comes undone it is because another one is being tied. When the book closes, the Caliph and Scheherazade make love (for the first time?). Much later, tired of happy endings, the Caliph orders her to tell him another story. She begins with the apocryphal Night, number 602: the story of the woman who must begin telling stories again. The Caliph laughs at her quick-wittedness and awaits a new story the following night. Before that can happen, Scheherazade escapes from the palace.

The Caliph, dining with some ambassadors from a distant land, has promised the guests that his wife will delight them with a marvellous story after pudding.

The two black guards glance at each other without a word as she slips out and heads into the desert. The moon is full, and her silhouette moves across the sand dunes.

Suddenly Scheherazade encounters Death, who is choosing the finest sand for his hourglass.

'There is a moment each night, the briefest instant', he says, without greeting or looking at her, 'when I carry no one off. It is when I am gathering sand for my hourglass. Each grain is a star. When all the grains have passed from one side to the other, when you've seen all the stars you're supposed to see, I will be waiting for you.'

'I haven't seen a single star for almost three years,' says Scheherazade.

'It's true. Three years ago, you were on the point of seeing the last star that had been allotted to you. But you began to tell stories. Now, it's easy. If you raise your head and gaze at the sky, you'll come with me tonight. Otherwise, lower your head, return to your room in the palace and tell this story. Tomorrow will be another day.'

In his final version of the *Variations*, Glenn Gould introduces a subtle, almost imperceptible change, breaking with the nocturnal circularity. As if he didn't want the Count to sleep after all, condemning Goldberg to inhabit that wakeful night forever. The change occurs in the last beat of the final aria: an ornament that concludes the recording.

In his essay on the translators of the *One Thousand and One Nights*, Borges enumerates at least nine. He pays particular attention to Burton's version of 1872, as well as to the most famous and possibly worst translation, the one by French orientalist Jean Antoine Galland, who seems to have added some of the jolliest stories – Aladdin and Ali Baba – with his own hand. These additions are now part of the canon. After all, the book is like a great paella dish to which everyone has added the best they have to offer. By definition, a classic dish is not signature cuisine.

Gould's great contribution lies not in what he modifies, but in the very gesture of modification.

Glenn Gould records his final version of the *Goldberg Variations* in the same studio where he recorded the first one. The first is just over thirty-eight minutes in length; the second is slightly over fifty-one. In that twenty-six year gap, he recorded everything that Bach ever composed for keyboards. It could be treated as one great piece of music. (Could we not do this for the oeuvre of any musician?)

In the thirty-fourth minute of *Sgt. Pepper's*, Night number 602 turns up: the Beatles begin to play the first song on the album, the title song, all over again. The song that follows, however, is not the second track on the album, but 'A Day in the Life': pure sound astronomy. We listen like Caliphs on the moon.

Did Goldberg ever feel an urge to escape the palace, never to return?

It once occurred to me to imagine a job that only demands a single hour of work each day. Just one hour, as long as it's fulfilled without fail. With holidays, of course. Twenty days including weekends. A Christmas bonus. All very nice. It could be a very simple task. One full hour, no messing around; doing some figures, let's say, or making holes in a wall. Nothing complicated. Painting. There's no Saturdays or Sundays, but one hour every day to do our work. The same time each day. Let's say nine to ten each morning, no need for early risers. Very well paid. For our whole lives. Isn't this, more than any other routine, the exact measure of time?

One night, long after he's cured of his insomnia, the Count will vaguely recall the variations Goldberg used to play. The melodies will jumble in his memory. Gout keeps him awake. Goldberg has left some time ago, Keyserling gifted him the scores. Regretting this gesture, he asks a palace musician to play the melody he hums tunelessly.

The Count gives up, annoyed, unable to remember the fragments of the variations.

How did Scheherazade express herself those first nights? With veils and pyrotechnics, perhaps, since she has an infinite handful of stories ahead of her.

She ages with each story, knowing that the sand is

running through her fingers.

Does the pace of her storytelling slow as the candles burn lower?

She'll no doubt be shrewd in the way she tells the tale. Though isn't it better to return to the verve of the first night – the Caliph favours younger women, after all – than to stagger into the last one, exhausted, welcoming death in like a long-lost daughter?

It's the mother's monotone lullaby that sends a baby to sleep.

In music, melody is like light: it occupies all our attention – higher, higher still.

For the baby to fall asleep quickly, the mother's singing should use as few notes as possible; the ideal is just two, otherwise the child continues to chase the light that languishes on its mother's eyelids.

Language always bores inwards: only when a child learns to speak does it realize that it dreams. And then day and night are no longer the same thing.

Today we know, thanks to studies of the REM phase, that even a foetus dreams.

And it can only dream in sounds: the beating heart of its mother.

Could a foetus dream that its mother's heart has stopped?

Impossible: it can't dream something it has never perceived.

The very persistence of a sound transforms it from figure to background.

Silence is the mother's heart beating.

Sound, whether dreaming or awake, is the mother's

heart beating.

Being outside and inside at the same time.

The Count tosses and turns in his bed. When did he last dream of that melody?

Scheherazade tells her story, and the Caliph rubs his head as if he were tired.

A future mother sleeps, her foetus too.

Perfect peace is a Russian doll, intact, made of milk.

Johannes Brahms' 'Wiegenlied' is probably the best-known lullaby after 'Rock-a-Bye Baby': a song that can be hummed without words, with the mouth closed, almost instinctively. Brahms composed it in 1868 for Hans, the second child of a Swedish soprano named Bertha Faber, with whom he'd had a fling as a young man. Apparently Bertha would whisper this melody, or part of it, to Brahms. The composer held onto it for years before offering it to the son of his former lover. Where had she got the melody from? What's most likely is that her mother sang it to her. The melody cradles the lovers, making them fleetingly one.

Brahms wrote a peculiar letter to the father of the child: 'You will realise that I wrote "Wiegenlied" for Bertha's son. You will have the impression that while she sings it to young Hans, someone is singing her a love song in turn.'

It's easy to imagine what follows. Such gratuitous sincerity left the man baffled and annoyed. The child in heaven and the father in hell when he hears Bertha crooning the melody.

But when she sings, where is she?

He forbids his wife from putting their child to sleep with that song.

The lullaby prowls his insomnia.

It's said the soprano sang it in public on several occasions. It was part of her repertoire when she knew her husband wasn't in the audience.

And so the 'Wiegenlied' became the most famous lullaby in the world.

And Hans, to whom it was dedicated, was the only child never to fall asleep to it.

There was a Leningrad grandmother who would tell the children a story before bedtime every night. It was always the same one, because kids don't like it when their stories change. One day – maybe of hunger, maybe of cold – the babushka died. And so another tried to take up the task. But she didn't know the story very well, so the children had to teach it to her. Night after night, they corrected it and perfected it together. There were fairies in the tale, and talking animals too. The city remained under siege by the Germans for 900 days.

Gould suffers from insomnia; he spends hours talking on the phone as though he's only able to communicate through pure sound. He pays no attention to time zones when he calls. More than once, his interlocutors have fallen asleep in the middle of his endless monologues. Today, it's thought he had a degree of Asperger's, perhaps because this is the cause ascribed to everything that wasn't accurately diagnosed at the time – that or being bipolar. Farther back, it would have been neurasthenia. In any case, we should imagine Gould night after night, staring out the window at the forest, not far from Toronto, with the receiver stuck to his ear and a woman on the other end to whom he's unable to utter a word when she's standing in front of him.

He sleeps with the radio on and can't understand two things: that people get annoyed by noise, by background music, while at the same time they love the band he once discovered by chance, The Beatles.

In the documentary *Glenn Gould's Toronto* we see its subject at the zoo, singing Mahler's 'Saint Anthony's Sermon to the Fish' to the elephants. It's an extraordinary scene, whichever way we look at it.

What, this fellow can conduct an orchestra of pachyderms, overflowing with joy, but he can't talk face-to-face with his own family?

The baby hears the mother's song drifting further and further away, until it reaches the moon.

A week since the nocturnal ritual began, the Count has become familiar with the pathway that leads him to sleep. This gives rise to a problem: when the signposts are there, it's hard to get lost in the woods. Perhaps he has to wait for the next variation, the one he doesn't know yet, before he can nod off. Once or twice, he asks Goldberg to begin with any one of them at random. But the ear is a hunter of phosphorescent sounds, and sleep is impossible to befriend.

When Goldberg sees the candelabrum approaching, its glow somewhere between the sun and the moon, he begins to play the aria. The Count has ordered that the *Variations* should only be performed in his presence, and only once he's in bed. He doesn't want to hear the music at any other time.

When is the last lullaby sung? It gradually fades away, just as we gradually shift into sleep — until one day, unknowingly, we sing our child their final lullaby. They've asked for it. Perhaps it's been a few nights already. We don't know that it's the last time, but our child does. It takes a while for sleep to come.

At one point the words to Brahms' 'Lullaby' say:

Sleep now blissfully and sweetly,
see Paradise in your dream.

Every so often, the news mentions some video uploaded to the internet that's been watched by millions in a short space of time, breaking unlikely records of the kind that are forgotten as soon as we stop paying attention, like a newspaper horoscope. When a baby appears on a screen, it's followed by an exclamation that expels all air from spectators' lungs, both women and men secure in their masculinity. The image of a baby is a kind of living mandala that momentarily dissolves us into the eternal present it inhabits. At what point do we stop gazing at or being enchanted by a child? At what age, if we're not the parent? Two years old, perhaps? By gazing I mean the mere fact of staring at a baby, not because it's doing anything particularly funny. Is it when we can understand what it's saying? Or on the day it stops being spontaneous, that is, when it learns to pretend? When its fragility dwindles and it no longer needs constant care? A baby is protected by everyone, a child by some, an adolescent by few; adults have to look after themselves. The species preserves itself; but there's something lacking in this kind of explanation, Darwinian as it is, because contemplating a baby means gazing at music in space.

Between 1901 and 1905, Gustav Mahler writes his *Songs on the Death of Children*. The final composition, much like a lullaby, ends like this:

They rest as if in their mother's house:
frightened by no storm,
sheltered by the Hand of God.

With a mother's superstitious fear, his wife Alma yells at him not to tempt fate.

Vasya, the valet, leaves the candelabrum on a table by the harpsichord. He listens, his eyes gazing into the darkness. He too knows the *Variations* pretty well by now. He can guess which one comes next. But he can't work out what the one he never gets to hear is like.

Variations on the name Scheherazade:
Shirazad
Shahrazad
Shahrizad
Şehrazat

The premiere of Brahms' 'Lullaby' was held on 22 December, 1869 in Vienna. It was sung by Louise Dustmann, accompanied by Clara Schumann – the composer's impossible love – on the piano.

In the middle of the night, when the lullaby has been heard for the last time, in that brief spell in which no one has died, the child feels two hearts beating in its dream.

In reality, it hears one; it knows two.

Vasya, the valet, leaves the candelabrum on a table by the harpsichord. His devotion prevents him from praying that the snores will take longer to come.

It's the sign that the Count is sleeping. A rumble of thunder that announces the coming dreamstorm.

Did Clara Schumann know the story of Brahm's 'Lullaby'?

This time Goldberg plays twenty of the variations before the Count drifts off. He must have been worried about something, he murmurs to the valet. Vasya shrugs, surprised. Could it be that the music, like all medicines, requires ever-stronger doses to produce the same effect?

Right at the end of *Sgt. Pepper's*, in the very last groove of the disc, once the E-major chord that concludes 'A Day in the Life' has faded away, we hear a series of unintelligible words in reverse. Like a mantra, the record needle remains stuck in this eternal wheel unless it's lifted off by hand.

Geertgen tot Sint Jans was a Dutch painter who died in 1490 at the age of thirty. His legacy amounts to just twelve works. At least two of them are truly astonishing: *The Glorification of Mary* and *Nativity*. Two sides of a coin – or of a record. *Nativity* is a nocturnal piece that seems to have been intended for private devotional

21

use, a kind of beautiful mandala inspired by the visions of Saint Bridget of Sweden, who in a rapture had seen the swollen, pulsating womb of the Virgin and, superimposed, a luminous baby in its cot – so bright that the sun appears pale and watery by contrast. The radiant silence of Geertgen's painting is the reverse of *The Glorification*. Here the God-child is seen in the arms of his mother, swinging two little bells as if possessed, surrounded by three choirs of angels, if that is what we can call the three circles around him. Cherubs and six-winged seraphs inhabit the innermost circle, which is yellow. The second is caramel-coloured and occupied by angels displaying the instruments of the Passion: cross, hammer, spear and nails. The third is black, and here is where things get seriously noisy: viols, lutes, trumpets, drums, hurdy-gurdies, bagpipes and horns, which have never played together in an orchestra, are all sounding in unison. The child looks up and to the right, to where an angel is shaking a set of bells just like his.

The God-child seems to be a little out of control.

A concert in heaven, a party for a little scamp who refuses to go to sleep; there's something jazz-like about it. Maybe because the angels look like the devils painted by Brueghel.

It's a charming painting. Above all because the child looks a bit wild and it's not hard to imagine him playing out of rhythm, or the angels trying to follow a syncopated, disarrayed, unpredictable beat.

Except for certain grotesquely kitsch images or New Age prints aimed at hearts of a cosmic sensitivity, no paintings ever show Christ smiling. Nor as a baby playing. His repertoire of actions is limited to sleeping or lying in his mother's arms, as placid as a little tree.

In this painting, the light doesn't emanate from the child. The light comes from the Virgin.

What lullaby did Little Nemo's mother sing to him?
We need a lullaby for the Seven Sleepers of Ephesus.
And another one for Rip Van Winkle.

When I was about eight years old my father bought a radio known as the Noblex 7 Mares. It was a supercomputer that, along with the bass and treble controls, had six buttons for tuning into the same number of bandwidths. The dial display was an amalgam of a rainbow and a musical score, and the needle a baton, or better still: a fishing rod.

A red button on the left lit up the universe, as long you kept a finger pressed on it.

With the Noblex 7 Mares, we could tune in to radio stations from around the world.

It must have happened on five or six evenings, that is to say, my whole childhood: after dinner we cleared the table and my father began to turn the dial. Turbulence, electrical storms, strange silences, crackling embers, whales and dolphins in chorus, faraway music – until we hit on a voice in a foreign language. Little Champollions trying to decipher its origin. Who knows what my father was deducing when he exclaimed *Germany!* Then we looked above the dial: inside the lid was a map of the world with the time zones, and yes, there was Germany. Our excitement lasted a few seconds, and then we cast the rod into the sea again. Thousands of kilometres traversed simply by moving the dial a couple of centimetres. It's strange, but in my memory the visual sensations are stronger than the audible ones: the colours of the dial, the little lights.

And the indestructible notion that my father could unearth even the best-concealed treasures.

23

Once, the Count wakes up at three in the morning. Darkness and an ancient silence, as if it had snowed. Might it be snowing? He strains his ears and opens his eyes. He turns his head towards the window: a dark egg, no moon; he turns back, his mind almost empty, and suddenly the first strains of the opening aria of the *Variations* appear before him. Then a few moments of nothing, before the melody starts up again *da capo*, and over and over those five or six bars that mark a little circular excursion leading nowhere. The Count remembers nothing of this nocturnal interruption the next day – not until he lies down again and Goldberg places his fingers on the keys.

Insomnia also afflicts Vasya. That morning in the kitchen, he hums to himself, tracing a fragment of the night across the sunlit tranquillity.

And at yet another of those soirées with tea and cakes, Goldberg is forced to switch the course of his improvisations, as his fingers begin to form the shape of that first aria of their own accord.

For forty-five minutes in 2007, the renowned violinist Joshua Bell performed, incognito, a series of Bach partitas at a Washington subway station during rush hour. The idea was to observe more or less scientifically the relationship between beauty, perception and our surroundings. The acoustics were excellent, and Bell had brought his 1713 Stradivarius. There is a video that shows how no one – apart from a woman with her child and a man who stops for a second as if returning – pays him the least attention, although a few toss him coins. Despite the dictates of common sense, Bell was taken aback. The background noise comes through loud and clear, like a half-finished canvas by Jackson Pollock.

'At one moment I heard playing in the distance, perhaps in a radio advert, a fragment of "Right Down the Line", a great song by Gerry Rafferty I listened to a lot as a teenager,' Bell later told a journalist from the *Post*.

Everything is dark and silent when the Count opens his eyes in the early morning.

Sometimes the Caliph awakens in the middle of the night and a suspicion begins to form: this woman is plotting something with all these stories.

And the husband of Brahms' lover jolts awake when he realises he's dreaming about that now-omnipresent song.

'How do you sleep?' Lennon asks McCartney in his song of this title, a track on the album *Imagine*. And he sings 'The only thing you've done was yesterday.'

There's something wrong with the *Variations*, thinks the Count, who is taking longer and longer to get to sleep.

Years later, Scheherazade's son wants his mother to tell him a story, but instead she sings him a lullaby, a looping melody about a child lost in the desert who comes running to where his mother awaits.

The Count won't remember waking up again during the night when Vasya comes to rouse him the next day, save for a dim recollection mid-morning when he thinks he hears one of the servants humming a tune that sounds much like the opening aria of the *Variations*.

Unlike the day, the night is always the same. That is why we dream.

Except Scheherazade's nights, which are always different. And the Count's are all alike.

Goldberg studies a score while two ladies drink tea. Can he hear one of them humming that opening aria?

Vasya, standing at Goldberg's side, silently begs for another variation, a new one, something to clear his head of the sleepless chords of the aria lodged there since early that morning, as he gave a couple of orders in hopeless German to the lad bringing the wineskins of milk for the tea drunk by the ladies, who are dazzled by the dexterity of a musician who cannot clear his head of the insistent bells that those first chords have become, keeping the Count awake, oppressing Vasya and forcing him to follow the same course as always down the keys of a clavier that is pretty well-tempered indeed, despite the inconstant temperature of the room.

McCartney dreamt the melody of 'Yesterday' so vividly that as soon as he woke up he switched on a tape recorder and played it on the piano, totally convinced it wasn't his. 'Eventually, it became like handing something into the police. I thought if no one claimed it after a few weeks, then I could have it.'

'Yesterday' is the most-performed song in history. Over 3,700 versions have been counted in every genre imaginable. And ever since its release in 1965, a radio station somewhere in the world has always been playing it, as if by tacit agreement among DJs.

Like there's always someone somewhere singing a lullaby.

And the white dove was sitting on a green lemon tree.

Lingering on the day before 'Yesterday', when McCartney finished gathering what the song would become in his dreams, the sunny day right before the rain is pouring and the old man's snoring. That penultimate day must have a consistency like the day when a song is played for the very last time.

At that moment, unnoticed by anyone, a song is heard for the last time before it returns to where it came from.

No more than fifteen years ago, a fisherman living on the River Yangtze unknowingly caught the very last Baiji dolphin after an exhausting struggle. We can only imagine his elation and his family's pride when he returned to his village with his catch. There was a feast of roast meat that night.

What melody died when 'Yesterday' was born?

Scheherazade's version of the tale of the golden ass was transformed when retold by a eunuch, and apparently now has a different ending.

Every day more occupants of the palace halt their chatter when they perceive, like crumbs falling, the first bars of the opening aria of the *Variations*. Then the conversation takes over again (Goldberg and Vasya are pretty sure that in the adjacent rooms people draw closer to listen).

This time, the Count falls asleep during variation number twenty, and both harpsichordist and valet head down to the kitchen to drink a cup of tea. There are no women around to entertain them; it is All Saints' Eve and these traditions are to be respected. Then Goldberg, looking for the sugar, comes across an open tin of coffee. Some impulse makes him sniff the sleeping Count's empty cup. There's a trace of coffee, he's sure of it. With a gesture he asks if the valet can smell anything odd, and the latter responds in Russian with a shrug of the shoulders. Well, it's none of his business after all, thinks the musician.

John Lennon composed two lullabies, one for each of his children. The first is sung by Ringo and is called 'Good Night'. This rather kitschy balsam closes the aleph that is the Beatles' *White Album*. The other one is 'Beautiful Boy', from his final album. That's where we learn that thing about life being what happens to us while we're busy making other plans.

One grey morning, Goldberg leaves the palace. It's a day of clouds and a polar cold. He walks through the village. A woman with a babe in arms is standing on a threshold, singing a lullaby. The musician unthinkingly passes her a coin, not realising it is one of the gold louis. That night the woman is sleepless with joy. If she were a Gypsy she'd read his palm and lie to him and regale him with talk of a long and happy life. The musician carries on his way; the melody in his head has been replaced by the poor woman's lullaby. It's a song with just a few notes and a simple repetition, and he wonders if he could transfer it to the harpsichord and present it as one of the

Variations. Wouldn't it be a great shortcut for the Count to get to sleep once and for all?

That evening Goldberg plays the poor woman's lullaby in the palace, improvising on it. Vasya listens from a distance. He thinks he recognises the melody; didn't his own mother sing it to him as a child? He approaches the harpsichord, smiles and says something unintelligible in Russian. Goldberg offers a graceful nod and tries to dazzle him with virtuoso flourishes.

The rhythm of a lullaby is one that a mother naturally discovers when she rocks her baby in her arms. It's the rhythm of a ship on a calm, dark sea. Every mother carries a Noah's Ark in her womb (after all, there are forty weeks of gestation and forty days of flood). We've all been the animals in the Ark before descending to the earth.

Nowadays, 'Yesterday' is a song only heard in random, incongruous settings: on the radio, at the gym, in the car. A lightning flash in the storm, a firefly on the asphalt. Jostling against the racket of the radio station and the machines and the car horns, we hear it as if for the first time. No one chooses to sit down and play 'Yesterday' in their living room.

It's like that impossible journey you never take because it's so nearby: walking along the pavement in front of your own house, from one corner of the block to the next.

No two lightning flashes are alike, after all.

'The tea tastes odd,' says Goldberg, clucking his tongue. 'As if it had a remnant of coffee in it.'

Vasya looks at him in surprise.

'Coffee?' he echoes, his voice a little higher than usual.

Chaplin, Hitler and Wittgenstein, born in April 1889 four and six days apart respectively, were all rocked to sleep to the sound of Brahms' 'Lullaby'.

There is a music that is tasted before it is played, a smoky aroma that comes from the kitchen: the lights go down before the concert has begun. Sometimes the song is sweeter because we are already savouring what we know is coming. There's a part in the first and fourth variations that the Count particularly likes. Sometimes he is anxious not to fall asleep before he's heard them.

Yet shouldn't we fall asleep knowing that we're better off not traveling to certain places, that we should leave them alone ahead of us, pulsating with promise, because only the failures, the insomniacs, make it all the way there?

The knowledge that there, at the end of the road, is something that will always be waiting for us.

That Russian doll.

Goldberg never had much trouble getting to sleep. Nor in finding a woman to accompany him.

Spokoynoy nochi.

SILENCES

The *Symphonic Poem for 100 Metronomes* is a work composed by György Ligeti in 1962. The furrowed brow of a non-specialist may be smoothed by simply calling it an *installation* instead of a *musical work*. Apparently, the face relaxes a little when the problem of the signifier is resolved. The piece has a visual element, instructing that the metronomes should be arranged in a pyramid shape and that the audience must only enter once the musicians have set them all running as simultaneously as possible. That is, the audience enters after the performance has begun. The poem lasts between fifteen and twenty minutes. What begins almost in unison gradually falls out of synch; there follow waves of overlaid rhythms, flocks of birds wheeling across the sky without colliding. As the instruments begin to slow, galloping horses emerge, typewriters on overtime, raindrops on tin roofs, the unending applause to a speech by Stalin. In this long-distance race of one hundred monochord voices, Bach fugue-style, the horses gradually fall away, the sun breaks through the clouds and the rain eases off, the typists abandon their offices, the Soviet sycophancy of a secretarial trio fades out until only the tick-tock of an alarm clock remains.

Just one.

At some point the ticking stops, though the metronome keeps moving.

A headless chicken.

The audience don't make a sound.

When the last metronome finally falls still, there's a sudden rush of applause, and it sounds just like horses galloping on asphalt, clandestine sewing machines, a pair of giant rattles, again rain and again sun; the offices empty out, the auditorium falls quiet little by little until the hall is in silence once more.

Three years before a depression long masked by the bourbon led him to open his veins in a bathtub in New York, Mark Rothko finished a painting dominated by a lethargic, watery yellow. It is untitled, like most of his works, but also unnumbered. It measures 170 by 104 centimetres. It could be considered a twilight work, if he had not already painted the very folds of the night on a series of near-monotone canvases for a chapel in Houston – now known as the Rothko Chapel and open to all religions. John and Dominique de Menil, a couple of French philanthropists who had fled the Nazis, had been impressed with the large, dark panels the painter had created for the Four Seasons restaurant in the Seagrams building, but which, with a socialist's guilt, he ended up donating to the Tate Gallery, having returned the advance on his commission. In any case, the chapel is a place of absolute stillness (as is to be expected in such places). Dominique de Menil is emphatic: 'The paintings are very silent, very tranquil, almost as if they weren't there.'

To disappear; that's the idea.

To get back to the work at hand. In the face of so much darkness lying in wait, the possibility of a new dawn in Rothko's spirit is the best way to understand his yellow painting. The Christie's catalogue described it as a kind of aborted rebirth, the fingerprint of a soul on the skids. The work was never put on show. It belonged to his wife, who held on to it for years without lending it to any retrospectives. It's a hard painting to curate, falling outside any series. In 1987 it was sold to a well-advised group of investors who paid almost two million dollars for it, before selling it for eleven million to an anonymous buyer at an auction in 1994. Throughout those years the painting was held in a secure warehouse. It only came up for air at the auction; from there it went on to another Wall Street warehouse, curiously enough on the block adjacent to the previous one. The identity of its new owner was never revealed. Four years later, it was put back on the market by Sotheby's. The hammer fell this time at twenty million, a new record for a Rothko. An expert reckoned that the price was excessive, given that the painting didn't appear to be finished. No matter, it was a superb acquisition for Harpers Investments. Extreme, secretive security measures were in place for the work's transfer to a new bank vault, just a few blocks away.

After all, the good thing about not being able to read music is being able to observe handwritten scores as if they were abstract paintings. Looking at the musicality and visual rhythm and imagining it coincides in some way with the real meaning. Like ships on the sea, the forms on the even-keeled waves of the staff. The noise in our head only fades away once the music begins to play.

The Navajo call their sand paintings *iikááh*, which literally means *places where the gods come and go*. They form a door to the other world, dwelling place of the untainted ones, the first beings. They come to restore lost harmony: a sick body, the outcome of a pointless massacre. In the 1940s, the Museum of Modern Art in New York invited a group of Navajo to create several paintings in coloured sand for the museum technicians to copy, with the intention of preserving this priceless cultural artefact.

The Navajo traced patterns with a startling purity, but always left a small area blank: this meant the drawings were incomplete. A double lock on the gates to the soul; a way to prevent the paintings from commencing their task.

Once the ritual is complete, the Navajo merge the colours into one, and collect the sand in little bags without saying a word.

These are emptied into a river, or left at the mercy of a red wind. Sometimes, they are kept.

The Navajo shamans are called *hatáli*, which means 'singers'; their voices activate the paintings.

The Tibetans do exactly the same thing with their sand mandalas.

I once received a little package from my cousin Paula on the occasion of a family event I was unable to attend. The envelope instructed me to open it with care. Inside was a letter: 'I don't why I've kept this little goblet amongst my most precious things for thirty years now. Your dad made it one New Year's Eve. Probably to get me to stop pestering him and let the grown-ups talk. There was something in his gaze that made me keep it to this day.' The letter went on. The little cup or goblet is fashioned from the metal foil that covers the neck of a cider bottle and is about five or six centimetres high. It suggests dexterity and determination. My father's hands were large, and its diminutive size must have required close attention. The stem forms a spiral before opening out into a base that stands up at a slight angle. A drunken cup. My family always came together for New Year's. This would have been after the toast. The gatherings were multitudinous and noisy. In each irregular fold, which could be transferred to a canvas in a few vigorous brush-strokes, I can see the delicacy of his rough hands. It's easy to work out how he made it. It can't have taken more than a minute. But that's not how we measure such things. He must have stopped listening to my cousin, getting her to close her mouth at last and open wide her blue eyes. I like to imagine that everyone fell silent at that moment. I doubt it.

Paula lived in many different places and always kept this little goblet with her.

Death takes Bach by surprise as he is writing *The Art of Fugue*. As a result the piece concludes with an abrupt gentleness, as if someone lying in bed had stopped breathing.

No serious recording of the piece ends with a flourish or a fade out. The musicians simply stop playing. For a first-time listener, it offers a clear foretaste of death's surprising indifference.

Glenn Gould performed it on the piano. He saw the final counterpoint as the 'most extraordinary piece that a human mind had ever conceived'. There, at the end, he comes to a sudden halt, raising his left hand abruptly and then lowering it like a tremulous question mark.

His body shaken by the electric lash of a whip.

Rothko became extremely obsessive when he was preparing for an exhibition. Viewers had to stand at least seventy centimetres from the paintings. Neither spotlights nor natural light were allowed. In his studio, a lethal darkness reigned, the windows always covered over.

He painted alone, without witnesses.

And his paintings couldn't be paired or share a gallery room with anyone else's.

A kind of womb; modal light. I've created a place, he told the critic Dore Ashton when she came to visit his studio.

In 1968 the visual artist Mary Bauermeister decides to settle with her two children in New York. She sends a reverse-charge telegram to her husband, the composer Karlheinz Stockhausen, informing him of a decision he never even imagined possible. Stockhausen is left cold as marble. She doesn't reply to any of his letters or telegrams. Discarding the idea of suicide, he embarks on a hunger strike with the aim of forcing her to return. During the seven days of his fast, confined in a devastating solitude, the composer writes a text called *Richtige Dauern*. It contains instructions for a performance:

Play a sound
Play it for so long
until you feel
that you should stop
(…)
Live completely alone for four days
without food
in complete silence, without much movement
(…)
After four days, late at night,
without conversation beforehand
play single sounds

WITHOUT THINKING which you are playing

Close your eyes
Just listen

The Beatles had already finished *Revolver* and Japanese soldiers from World War Two were still being discovered defending deserted islands in the Pacific Ocean, buried in impenetrable jungles. These soldiers weren't frozen in time; rather, they had come to the point of greatest tension that life has in store for us, before returning, like an elastic band recovering its shape, further and further back until they reached those very first mornings. Dwellers in stillness; attentive to the slightest sign of an omnipresent enemy; lacking any instrument to play music with.

A starving dog on alert.

A twenty-five-year-long day.

There were many such cases of lost Japanese soldiers. There were three million soldiers in the Pacific, after all.

Of course, we only know about the ones who were found.

The body becomes autonomous: it regulates thinking.

And a regulated thought is anything but a thought.

The last Japanese soldier to be found was called Hiroo Onoda. The band from Liverpool had already split up four years before that happened.

Sometimes Scheherazade falls silent and lowers her head, as if searching for the right word. It lasts a couple of seconds, like the trill of a blackbird; before continuing she exhales, a faint sigh easily perceived by an attentive ear. Is it possible to love a person incapable of noticing that? How many more nights?

In the final scene of the film *The Conversation*, Harry Caul destroys his apartment in a fury of thoroughness. He begins by tearing up an image of the Virgin Mary, then goes on painting by painting, ornament by ornament, even lifting every single piece of the parquet floor. The camera pans through the apartment-turned-Hiroshima; we see him sitting with his back against a wall he has stripped of its wallpaper. A soft lament begins on the sax. Harry Caul is a detective and an expert in secret recordings. He only cares about the quality, not the content. He's the best, it seems. Someone has hidden a microphone in his own apartment and he's been sent the recording.

Harry Caul has a Japanese soldier in his apartment, and he's still at war.

In 2004 the yellow Rothko is purchased by a British investment firm. It is transported to London and stored at Barclays Bank.

When he reaches the end of the *Goldberg Variations*, Glenn Gould lifts his fingers from the keys, but not his wrists; he lowers his palms, raises them again, and abruptly lifts his hands away as if the keys were burning hot. His palms end up perpendicular to the piano, as if saying *Enough*. Gould is hunched over, as always. He drops his hands to his lap and bows his head. It's like he's curling up into the foetal position.

In 1893 Erik Satie composed a 150-note work called *Vexations*. The score indicates that it should be played 840 times in a row and that, therefore, 'it would be advisable to prepare oneself beforehand, and in the deepest silence, by serious immobilities.'

It was performed for the first time in 1963 at the Pocket Theatre in New York. The concert was organised by John Cage. Fourteen pianists, including Cage himself, played the piece for more than eighteen hours. Only one person made it through the entire performance without falling asleep, an actor at the Living Theatre by the name of Karl Schenzer. He worked on Coppola's first film, *Dementia 13*, and his work as a private detective later inspired the director to write the story of *The Conversation*. The performance was also attended, at least in part, by Andy Warhol and John Cale.

However incredible it may seem, Schenzer was unable to recall the melody to *Vexations* after just a couple of days, yet he could bring to mind certain sequences of ambient noises he'd heard in the theatre.

Stockhausen hears only birds during that week of fearful solitude. Birds and his own weeping, we may imagine.

And he paces around and around the room.

In the first, great scene of *The Conversation*, Harry Caul is followed around a city square by a mime.

On Tokyo nights, Iori Kishaba, a Japanese soldier who had been posted to an island for thirty years, stares through the window of his hotel as the lights come on in a city that no longer sleeps. Little suns on the vertical sea of cement. Tomorrow, there'll be medals and a toast. He thinks about his solitary island and the silence broken only by the waves.

As part of their courting repertoire, male whales emit warm songs in a range between 15 and 25 Hz. Pleasant and somehow tender as they are to the human ear, there's always someone who adds soda water to good wine: there are countless recordings of whale music layered over predictable new age violins. Urban nirvana in salt water.

It's likely that whale antiphonies have another function beyond mating rituals; perhaps they serve to mark out territories. In 1990 the Wood Hole Oceanographic Institution located a song with a very, very high frequency, at least for a whale: 52 Hz. A real oddity. Today we know that it belongs to a whale that travels around the northern Pacific, from the Aleutians to the coast of California. The song is so high-pitched that even its peers can't hear it. Theories abound: the whale may be deaf, or the last member of an unknown species. Whatever; its loneliness, in any case, is unending. Inevitably, there are young and enthusiastic film directors, Adrian Grenier and Josh Zeman, ready to make a documentary.

A castrato's fate: the loneliest whale in the world doesn't follow the migration route of any other cetacean. Apparently, its voice is getting a little deeper every year, as if it had intuited the right path to follow.

A whale song can be heard at a distance of 5,000 kilometres. That's the distance between Buenos Aires and Caracas, or Moscow and Barcelona.

Whales, too, mourn for their dead.

It took seventy-five years for the audience at the Bayreuth Festival, dedicated solely to Wagner operas, to applaud sopranos, basses and tenors. The first ovation was heard in 1951. Before then, not even the conductors bowed at the end of the performance. Only the work itself was celebrated (after all, who applauds a priest after delivering mass?) The theatre had been built especially to host Wagner's work, and was left unscathed by the Allied bombing of the small city where it stands. The 'silence of Bayreuth' is the name given to the impenetrable barrier that begins when the lights go down, a couple of minutes before the curtain is raised, and ends a minute after the performance is over. No one sneezes, no one coughs, no one does anything. That's how it's been since 1876. 'You seem to sit with the dead in the gloom of a tomb,' wrote Mark Twain of his visit.

The thing Glenn Gould hated most about performing was the applause. He saw it as an immoral, automatic reaction; insincere, at best. At a concert where he played *The Art of Fugue* he asked the audience to refrain from clapping, and for the lights to gradually fade to darkness in the final phrases, as a sign of reverence. He later wrote an article in which he unveiled the 'Gould plan for the abolition of applause and demonstrations of all kinds.'

Objects torn from their present; shouldn't we gather the sand before its grains become merchandise?

Treating something as merchandise means to inscribe it in time: to see it as future profit, as an investment, as a cost to be recovered. Seeing it as itself means removing it from the flow of time, returning it to the mute fire from which it came. Navajo sand.

Iori Kishaba would always go to a particular stretch of beach at sunrise. He prayed every day for the health of the emperor.

When Jackson Pollock was asked about the influences on his gestural style, his list included the Navajo paintings he had seen in 1940 at the Museum of Modern Art in New York. Finding yourself within the painting as you work on it is something that pertains to these cultures, he added. When the photographer Hans Namuth took the famous series of images showing the painter at work, he recalled that upon entering his studio 'A dripping wet canvas covered the entire floor... There was complete silence... Pollock looked at the painting. Then, unexpectedly, he picked up can and paint brush and started to move around the canvas.' What followed was a shaman dance lasting almost an hour, during which the artist didn't even notice the presence of the photographer and his assistant.

Geneva, Singapore, Luxembourg: all places where works of art no one ever contemplates are kept in storage. Goyas, El Grecos, Picassos. Swarms of Impressionists. A whole ocean where clients often forget all about the fish they contain. Secure rooms, discreet personnel. They're called Free Ports. Such a dense concentration of art in so few square metres means that insurance companies don't even dream of placing bets on it.

The Caliph cannot forgo his tradition of killing a concubine each night: weakness is unseemly to a great Lord. When Scheherazade falls silent, she feigns a smile and glances sideways at the others present; sometimes she asks for wine. How many more nights must this siege go on, she wonders.

In a sensory isolation chamber, the nearest thing to a uterus we've ever created, we can only hear two sounds, on different wavelengths. The low sound is our blood pumping; the other is our nervous system. This was the explanation John Cage received when he asked about the two noises he'd heard inside.

It's impossible to hear total silence. The same thing goes for temperature. Absolute zero, where all particles are at rest, is unattainable.

Two hundred and seventy-three degrees below zero.

Two hundred and seventy-three seconds is the length of John Cage's work *4' 33"*, performed for the first time by pianist David Tudor to a packed house.

A premiere of roles reversed: the stage is noiseless; all sounds come from the auditorium.

Once the piece was over, Tudor stood up and bowed to the audience.

Who, disconcerted, finally stopped their murmuring.

No one clapped, of course.

The *Funeral March Composed for a Deaf Man*, by Alphonse Allais, could well be a forerunner of *4' 33"*, though it is more like a painting than any other art form, as the silences are not even marked on the score. Unlike Cage's piece, the *March* was not intended to be performed.

Allais had already created a series of monochromatic

works. *First Communion of Anaemic Girls in the Snow* of 1883 would appear to predate Malevich's white square. But total silence can't be possible there, not with such a figurative title.

At absolute zero, atoms come together in a chewing-gum totality. Let's just say that in this treacle things don't behave the way they're supposed to.

All elements freeze except for helium – the distant sun of helium – which reaches a state of matter known as superfluidity. *Exuent* Gravity, stage left.

At this temperature nothing vibrates. The silence is total. That's why there's no way of recording it.

Shoichi Yokoi lived in a cave on the island of Guam for twenty-eight years. He'd read the pamphlets that the Yankee planes had dropped, declaring the surrender of Japan and the end of the war. It was the only written inscription he saw for almost three decades. The second was the bronze plaque his mother had sent to be made in 1955 when she'd reached a different certainty. And it is beneath this plaque, in Nagoya cemetery, that his body has lain since 1987.

The Frenchwoman Éliane Radigue, who looks beautiful in photographs taken at any age, is among the greatest composers of electronic music. Her most delicate piece may be *Resonant Island*. It opens with a very low sound that advances without pause before very gradually expanding its spectrum, growing more high-pitched without losing its original depth (the image is of an expanding ripple). After exactly ten minutes, a soprano voice enters from what feels like the far side of the wind. The sounds solidify: it feels like all the world's instruments are murmuring. Fortunately, the New Age effect is abruptly cut off by the voice's sea-song, which could be mistaken for a sound that continues without pause.

Deeply influenced by the *Tibetan Book of the Dead*, Radigue embraced Buddhism when she was devastated by the death of her son Yves. This event inspired her to compose her masterwork, *Trilogie de la mort*. As if advancing through a space as slowly as the sea at night: that's how Éliane moves. A dorado fish that pops its head out of the water in vain: there's no one on the islands, no campfire.

The changes in timbre are incredibly subtle.

One by one, more fish gather, relentlessly.

Éliane is the shoal; an island on the move.

And so her head rests both in and out of the water until the piece comes to an end.

When Iori Kishaba returns home, the first thing he does is visit his own grave. There are no flowers. Just an austere plaque recording his presumed death. Kishaba bows his head and weeps. Beside it is the grave of his mother, who outlived him by fifteen years. Now, he is the one to have survived his mother.

In his parents' house he finds a few letters that his mother never sent, for fear of not receiving a reply. In one, she tells him about the beautiful black crows that caw in the afternoons. In another, she replies to an imaginary letter from her son. A third brings news of a birth in the family. She never reports any bad news. There is another letter with a poem. Perhaps of her own composition?

And as if he were running in a relay race against death, Kishaba decides to publish them. But only once he himself is dead: his brother will take care of the practical details. This is his final wish: to give his mother a voice. The two or three letters that had reached him were left behind on the island. The letters were published in 1983 in a short volume that was not widely distributed, never reprinted, and is impossible to find today. When we read these letters it becomes clear that the relay race has ended for them both: mother and son rest in peace together. It is we, the readers, who are on the island now.

Due to his wife's illness, the pianist Claudio Arrau was only able to fly to Amsterdam from his home in New York on the day of the performance. After landing he checked into his hotel, got changed and went straight to the concert hall without a chance to rest. His plan was to head back to New York the next day to be by his wife's side. Postponement was out of the question since the concert was part of a series of official celebrations. The pianist's friendship with Bernard Haitink, chief conductor of the Royal Concertgebouw Orchestra, had helped to smooth things over. They agreed that orchestra and pianist would rehearse separately. After all, it wasn't the first time they were playing Beethoven together. Just the previous year, in 1965, they had recorded the fourth and fifth concertos for Phillips Classics. So each set about preparing their respective parts of the performance.

Arrau's solo rehearsals gained in brilliance and colour in line with his wife's recovery. When her health plateaued without further improvement, his mood would falter too; his fingers would take on a life of their own, which is to say that his mind was elsewhere. A rather soulless Beethoven was the upshot. Happily, the very day before his flight, his wife showed marked improvement. She would be out of hospital the day of the concert. Arrau flew to Holland in infectiously high spirits.

The Dutch King and Queen were attending the concert, naturally.

Beethoven's Piano Concerto No. 4 begins with a piano solo, and the rest of the orchestra enters after this brief introduction.

In the Concerto No. 5, known as the 'Emperor Concerto', it is the orchestra that opens the piece with a powerful chord, before the piano enters.

Arrau and Haitink stride onto the stage and bow at the applause. (They've barely had the chance to exchange a few words in the dressing rooms about the condition of Arrau's wife. They'll speak later at the gala dinner.)

Arrau sits down at the piano and observes Haitink.

Haitink looks at the orchestra, turns his head and watches Arrau.

Arrau is certain that the concerto they are about to play is the fifth, which begins with the orchestra.

Haitink has prepared Concerto No. 4, the one that opens with the piano.

Pianist and conductor hold each other's gaze. At first, they are both smiling.

The loneliest whale in the world has been detected every year since 2004.

Hiroo Onoda recounted that once, on the Tokyo subway, his eyes had met the gaze of someone seated like him, hands resting in his lap, and scrutinising him with a ghost of a smile on his lips. Onoda acknowledged him with a bow of the head. Then the carriage filled with passengers, and they could no longer see each other. Onoda believes the man was Iori Kishaba, or someone who looked very much like him, judging by the photographs that had appeared in the papers. They never crossed paths again, if indeed they did on that occasion.

Stockhausen paces the room looking for an explanation. Yet some things aren't solved through reason alone. Reasoning means advancing in a straight line, while the body instinctively walks in circles. At some point the tangent – that point of silence at which reason and unreason converge – must be found and followed. But Stockhausen turns in such tight circles that he fails to glimpse the exit, even though he had passed it the day before, and the day before that.

Time and again, turning around the same thing.

And his wife in New York with their children.

In 2013 the yellow Rothko appeared once more at an auction. It was purchased by an anonymous telephone bidder. It has not been seen since.

Shoichi Yokoi said that he once saw a pod of dolphins pass by the beach in the mid-morning, under a cold and milky sun.

Bach never specified which instrument *The Art of Fugue* was written for. He arranged it on four different staves, not clarifying, either, the order in which its eighteen counterpoints should be played. In a sense, it might be called music without a timbre – or without sound, which amounts to the same thing, as if it didn't even need to be played. A visual music, in a manner of speaking, free from the impurities of the air. Something similar happens with certain kinds of conceptual art: the execution appears to take away from the idea.

But the idea alone is not enough.

When a baby is born, it has the power to speak every language in the world. Its mother's voice is pure music of the sweetest, mildest pitch. Yet day by day this almost monotonous lulling sound puts to sleep all the languages it will now never be able to speak perfectly. That's when the mother's voice stops being music: when words can be distinguished, meaning arrives, and the silence retreats, little by little, to let in the first thoughts. And so, the dead languages become a kind of toneless music, heard as if tracing a line across a canvas by Jackson Pollock.

Gazing at the score of *The Art of Fugue*, what sound rings out inside a musician's head? Perhaps it's something indefinite, like the voices we attribute to characters in a comic strip – together with the disappointment when we hear them in an animation.

The greatest sufferings are always silent, wrote Alphonse Allais with regard to his *Funeral March*.

And so, just as Stockhausen finds the point where circle and straight line converge, he runs out of words.

He raises the lid of the piano and plays a single note.

The first sound in his entire life, is what he says it feels like.

Empty, and emptied out.

His pain no longer matters to him, nor knowing if his wife will return or not.

He opens the window and the room is flooded with the scent of an orange tree in bloom.

In Mollar, a village near Tafí del Valle in the province of Tucumán, the outstanding musician Miguel Ángel Estrella arrives with his piano for a second time and begins to play Bach. The locals tell him that's very nice, that's fine, but could he please play that clear, pure music from the first time.

'Play that clear, pure music.'

So Miguel Ángel Estrella plays the Mozart rondo from his first visit.

And they ask him to repeat it.

And again.

And once again.

He plays that rondo twenty-two times in a row.

Monkeys in the sky with diamonds.

Actually they're all just one monkey.

But it was for this very reason – because his music carried people to the heavens – that Estrella soon went to hell in a Uruguayan prison. It was 1977. He'd escaped from Argentina by a whisker. The colonel in charge of the interrogation said to him: 'You're no guerrilla fighter, you're worse than that: with your piano and your smile you have the whole rabble in your pocket, giving the riff-raff the idea they can listen to Beethoven.'

And so the torture is focused on his hands. Simulations of amputations with an electric saw.

Torture with no practical objective. No possible confession.

International pressure, from Yehudi Menuhin to the Queen of England, helped to get a piano delivered to the prison.

But the military officers disconnected the hammers.

The piano was left silent. Mute.

An instrument of torture that leaves no marks and destroys the mind.

In the cell, the noises are deafening. Miguel Ángel Estrella is able to identify twenty-two different timbres of voices, the same as the number of times he played that Mozart rondo.

'I heard the cries of a woman they were raping or torturing with electric shocks, and my other self would tell me: "She's a contralto." Or: "This one's a soprano," "That's a tenor," "The guy next door is a baritone."'

Amidst the torture, his own cries also disappear. In one ear he hears the voice of his wife telling him he isn't alone; in the other, his teacher Nadia Boulanger begging him to hold out.

In a pavilion holding political prisoners in the Devoto jail in Buenos Aires, militants are locked up alone or in pairs with nothing to help them cling to the outside world: no letters, books or other souvenirs to accompany the colourless, unbroken confinement and halt their mental meandering. Yet they can hear a chorus from the other pavilions (a single voice wouldn't make it from one block to another) singing folk songs, some pop melodies, perhaps something by La Joven Guardia.

One of the prisoners is Elba, a beautiful black woman from Tigre, and one of the few whose partner is locked up in the same jail. She loves him furiously and sings like a dream. One day she makes a kind of trumpet out of paper to direct her voice straight into her man's ears.

She sings 'Nostalgias'.

And a total silence falls, even among the guards.

With the aim of creating an unbreakable code, the US Navy pursued an idea worthy of an adventure novel: they used the Navajo language in the war in the Pacific. The notion was greeted with scepticism, because the Navajo lack military terminology. Besides, they're Indians, of course. In the end, a total of 420 Navajo were recruited.

The code was never put into writing.

In the field of battle, the Americans confused their own Indians with the Japanese as they found their faces too alike, meaning the Navajo had to be accompanied by bodyguards. The Japanese never succeeded in deciphering the whistling noises they hunted down with their radios. The sound has been compared to the Tibetan monks' call to prayer.

A statement by Estrella's lawyer at a conference held in Paris in 1978: 'Migel Ángel is going mad, because he can only study with a mute piano, which is a veritable instrument of torture. He cannot synchronize the movement of his fingers, his hearing and the mental image. He is his own powerless witness to the total disintegration of his mental system.'

There was a prisoner in the Bergen-Belsen concentration camp who would listen intently to what another prisoner had to say in the two hours they were allowed to speak. And when he opened his mouth it was to ask about insignificant details of the other's family stories, which were always marvellous. The listener's fate was never known, just as no one remembers his name, if in fact he ever gave it. The few survivors who spoke of him couldn't describe any distinguishing feature. He was just like the rest of us. But silent.

Estrella is released from prison. Many years later, he returns to Tafí del Valle, and to Mollar. The people welcome him dancing in the streets. Dancing, with no music.

A woman approaches.

Please, she says, play that clear, pure music.

Many of those who attended the premiere of *4' 33"* couldn't help making smilingly indignant remarks. From time to time one would fall into silent thought.

During the performance, John Cage was alert to sounds: 'You could hear the wind stirring outside during the first movement. During the second, raindrops began pattering the roof, and during the third the people themselves made all kinds of interesting sounds as they talked or walked out.'

David Tudor, the pianist, never reported what went through his mind during the performance.

A solemn interpretation of the piece appears in a video by Bill Marx, son of Harpo, the silent Marx Brother.

In April 1945 the Allies bomb the German town of Halberstadt. Many people take shelter in a small Romanesque church built in 1050. After housing Trappist monks for 600 years, it functioned successively as a granary, distillery, warehouse, pig farm. Whistling as they fall, the bombs will remain lodged in the intact eardrums of a few children huddled under a round arch. Sixty years later, two of them will stand under the same arch to observe a musician hang three small bags of sand from the keys of an organ that, for the time being, has just five pipes. The sound will continue indefinitely until someone takes them off again, of course. They don't know which chord it is that begins to play, but they are sure of one thing: the nocturnal aeroplanes will never be coming back.

Navajo sand.

Scheherazade's sand.

In 1985 John Cage composed the work *ASLSP*, with the instruction that it should be played *As SLow aS Possible*.

Two years later, he worked on a piece for organ. The score is eight pages long.

Gerd Zacher prepared a version that is twenty-nine minutes long. The directions given by Cage, who was present in the auditorium, were that it should be played like 'a gentle morning' and that at the end 'it should disappear'.

Years later, a conference of musicians, theologians and philosophers came to the conclusion that the longest possible time is that of the useful life of an organ, or until the harmony of a society breaks down.

And for this new performance, the town of Halberstadt was chosen because that's where the first modern organ was constructed in 1361. The first one with twelve notes per octave (which suggests that the space of music opened up before that of painting.)

The concert began on 5 September 2001. Six days later the Twin Towers fell. It will continue for 639 years, seven more than it took to build Cologne Cathedral.

Each movement will last seventy-one years.

As in Beethoven's Symphony No. 5, the first note of *ASLSP* is a rest.

Seventeen months passed before the first sound was heard. The church remained open for anyone who wanted to await it there.

Festivities are held on the occasion of each chord change. At the time of this writing, the next change will take place on 5 September, 2020.

Once we arrive at the beach, the sound of the sea takes about ten minutes to disappear. After that it can only be found inside seashells. The same thing happens when we enter the Halberstadt church. The only ones who always hear the organ music are the two children who had taken shelter there and, at the age of eighty, will be in charge of moving the bags of sand to change the chord. Or to renew the silence.

Mothers have sung *The white dove was sitting on a green lemon tree* to their children for over a thousand years. Every single day, since at least the time of El Cid.

In Mark Applebaum's piece *Tlön (for three conductors and no players)* the conductors in question begin by gesturing the way sailors do, waving little flags to send signals, before each one picks up their baton and starts to conduct their own invisible orchestra. They all use the same score, but it becomes clear that they have determined the tempo and character individually. Towards the end, the conductors look at each other for the first time, the batons fall still and their open left hands make a few very soft, slow gestures.

The poet Hugo Mujica once related how, walking through the woods around the Trappist monastery where he spent three years living in silence, he crossed paths with an old monk. It was deep into autumn and getting late. The two monks advanced slowly with their hands folded in front of them. Mujica nodded his head in gentle greeting. The old monk gazed at him with the transparency of someone who can distinguish flavours in pure spring water.

'We're putting too much salt in the food,' he said, in jovial caution.

Mujica opened his mouth in astonishment.

The old monk closed his, and winked at him.

It was only a long time later that Mujica realised that the monk hadn't broken the rules at all.

Though we can memorise instrumental music, it is almost impossible to learn an abstract painting by heart. We remember sequences of things, not simultaneities. We can follow the traces of colour that stand out most clearly, which are something like the melody of the piece. It's as hard as knowing where a running child's next step will fall.

(Children listen to music in order to fall asleep.)

Once we know that, there is nothing more to be learnt.

Rothko would be a great name for a rock group.

Glenn Gould: the pianist doesn't play the piano with his fingers, but with his mind.

The town of Halberstadt is also home to an ornithology museum with a collection of 20,000 stuffed birds.

We can remember someone's face, but we are unable to isolate a fragment of it, such as the form of an eye − except, of course, in the case of people we live with, that is, those with whom we communicate without words.

There are no animals.

There is a power, or whatever we want to call it, that neither increases nor diminishes.

All the power of all the animals in the world is exactly equivalent to that of the first living cell.

There's nothing more than this. No new matter has been created since the Big Bang.

And this power takes the form of a giraffe or a jellyfish, swallows itself up, recreates itself, flees itself, alienates itself, becomes a mouth that wants to bite itself. Everything is pain and pleasure at once.

Something similar happens with music.

Nor are there plants.

The monk's steps
Water falling on dirty dishes
Bells
A crow
The pages of a book turning
The wind
A creaking chair
Distant hammering
A glass set down on the table
A rake drawing a spiral in the sand garden
Birdsong, faintly
A crow
A match
Coughing
A saw
Someone sighing
Sudden rain
Steps in the passageway
A crow
A glass set down

The smell of damp
A lemon tree
Sawing
A drawn curtain
All of this silence is heard in the abbey

That little dent above the lips no one knows the name of because it serves no purpose and doesn't tend to suffer injury is called the 'philtrum'. It is formed when the embryo develops pharyngeal arches; that is, it takes shape when we're fish. The ear structure begins to form at almost the same time.

Before we're born, according to a Jewish legend, there is nothing we don't know, but then an angel places its index finger on our lips so that we fall silent and forget. That's how the philtrum is formed.

Only those who are born without a belly button, like Adam, are born without a philtrum. That is why Adam doesn't keep quiet and goes around naming everything.

What's for sure is that there's no music in paradise.

THE GREAT ORGAN OF
HIMMELHEIM

The construction of the largest organ in the world –
indeed the biggest musical instrument of all time – began
in October 1737 and was initially the rather hazy vision
of Baron Gustav von Leyendecker, in whose lands, at the
foot of the Alps not far from Salzburg, lay the small town
of Himmelheim. The organ was inaugurated fifteen years
later on the occasion of the town's patron saint's day. The
Baron's original idea was to install a vast instrument that
could play at a greater volume and with more colour than
a symphony orchestra, if such a thing could be imagined.
Its construction, meanwhile, demanded the involvement
of all the townsmen: a true communion of souls that
would doubtless find an ally in the Bishop of Salzburg
when it came to covering the costs. If the image had come
to him in dreams, perhaps it would have been clearer
to everyone, above all to the gentlemen and architects,
carpenters and other craftsmen he had convened one day
to explain the project. Gustav von Leyendecker spoke to
them of a machine bursting with crank handles, pedals,
cogs, ramps, pegs. Then he told them about the sound. He
said that it must not be homogenous and constant but
rather, according to the instructions and certain delicate
mechanisms he found it impossible to describe, sometimes
a wind-sound should dominate, sometimes the sound of

strings. Everyone listening was left imagining some kind of demented music box with an erratic timbre. He then specified that a general conductor would give his orders from a twenty-metre tower, and at least four deputy conductors would be located on a succession of balconies. Only they would be required to be able to read music, while everyone else need only follow their instructions. The Baron was unable even to produce a coherent sketch on paper, with the result that everyone else understood little or nothing of his plans. Nevertheless, his enthusiasm did not falter as the morning wore on; instead, in his effort to clarify his ideas, the crank handles and frameworks disappeared and the complicated mechanisms gave way to pipes, bellows and keyboards, which led, in the end, to the manufacture of an absolutely colossal organ. At that point, everyone got excited.

As is true of venison, some ideas work better in literature than in cuisine.

It took fifteen years to build the instrument, and everyone wanted to have a hand in its construction, even if only to adjust a screw. The organ was to be the emblem and pride of the town, and no one wanted to be left out of the enterprise. Costs were covered by tax hikes and an exorbitant loan from a bank headquartered in Vienna.

To achieve as clear a sound as possible, the alloy used to make the pipes contained more tin than lead. The largest measured as much as twenty-five metres in length, and in total they numbered almost 15,000, including the flue pipes and reed pipes, and the so-called stopped pipes that, with their closed ends, can achieve the lowest sounds of all. There were seven manuals with ivory keys; the valves, the stops and the stop rods were made from the finest ebony.

Brillo, brillo! exclaimed the Baron as he clenched his fists and contemplated his pyramid growing day by day.

It was self-evident that such an enormous instrument could not be installed in the modest church of Himmelheim (nor even in the largest in the Empire, for that matter). Instead, a church would have to be constructed around it. That would be dealt with later. For the time being, a kind of monumental pergola had been built to protect it from the rain and snow.

People from neighbouring villages, eager to view its progress, began arriving in such numbers that a Sunday fair was created. One way or another, it was turning out to be a very good business that made everyone happy.

Despite the inevitable contretemps that befall all such great enterprises, the organ was finally completed without major setbacks.

The Kapellmeister of Munich had composed a choral prelude for its inauguration, accompanied by his cathedral choir. But when he arrived in Himmelheim and saw the great size of the organ, he realised his error. The sound of the instrument would undoubtedly drown out the human voices. So that night, at the inaugural banquet, he announced to the Baron that he had decided to change the programme. He proposed performing a series of preludes and fugues and ending with a fantasia that would allow him to improvise and explore the instrument's range of possibilities. The Baron assented; after all, he was not the expert. The members of the choir put on a performance at the end of the meal, justifying their journey. Their voices were truly marvellous. Many of them didn't go to sleep that night, heading instead to one of the town's three taverns. The exaltation of the beer – everyone was excited about the concert the next day – contrasted with the icy silence of those walking like pilgrims to the outskirts of the city, eager for a glimpse of the organ that night. The good weather had permitted the dismantling of the temporary roof that afternoon, and the light of the waxing moon ascended the pipes until the eye could follow no more. The organ gave the impression of truly reaching the heavens. A few visitors even kneeled and crossed themselves.

The next day dawned cold. Crowds gathered early. They drank coffee and ate warm pastries distributed by the Baron's lackeys. By mid-morning, every soul in Himmelheim was awaiting the concert. The town would have been a sitting duck for thieves, if the thieves hadn't been there too, eating pastries and drinking coffee.

At the expected hour the Baron delivered a stirring speech.

Everyone applauded, moved.

The bishop blessed the organ (droplets of holy water bespattered the console).

Then the Kapellmeister of Munich stood up. He bowed to the authorities in attendance, as a chamberlain hurried to adjust his chair. A forest-like silence descended. If the sun had fallen directly on the pipes, many people would have been blinded by the reflections.

Although the organ had been tested the previous autumn, and its timbre and volume had left everyone speechless, no one was truly prepared for what came next.

The Kapellmeister played a chord in A minor.

Followed by one in B minor.

And the sound not only seemed to expand from the instrument into everywhere at once, but also thundered in their chests as if someone were shaking them from the inside. Everyone was vibrating.

The sound inundated everything. It ricocheted off the mountains. The organ was redoubled by an Alpine reply.

Brillo, brillo! The Baron's eyes were wide, his fists clenched.

A deep rumble came from the mountains. This was no echo: it was a monstrous avalanche.

All those who could ran for their lives.

The snow buried the organ of Himmelheim.

And it buried the little town of Himmelheim.

For days, clouds covered the sun and the cold did its wintry work. The snow didn't begin to melt until a week later, once all the curious visitors from nearby towns were gone. The first to melt was the snow that had accumulated inside the organ pipes, while it was still piled deeply on the keyboards. And so the organ began its slow euphoria. As the pipes gradually freed themselves of snow, its volume and splendour grew. And then it would snow again, and some pipes would be stopped up.

Music was falling from the heavens.

At first, only the very tips of the largest pipes were visible, and barely.

The people of Himmelheim had taken refuge in the surrounding villages (and it seems that the Baron had found consolation in a Viennese palace).

With trepidation, people approached to hear this tuneless hymn. And when the sun unblocked more pipes and the volume rose, they withdrew in fear of another avalanche.

Spring-like days finally arrived, the snow on the console melted and the organ fell silent forever.

Orders came from Salzburg to dismantle it: a heavy snowfall could transform the instrument into a veritable avalanche machine. Craftsmen took it apart piece by piece and everything that could be put to a new use was carried away. The pipes were melted down and made into swords.

As the years passed, a forest grew up where the small town of Himmelheim had once stood, and it became a favoured place for the nobility to hunt red deer.

WARS

The theatre is full. No admission has been charged, for the simple reason that no one has any money, or even anything in their pockets to barter. A few days ago, the oboist Ksenia Matus sent her instrument to be repaired for the first of the three rehearsals. Just bring me a kitten, the maker said when they tried to agree on some form of payment, they're tastier than chickens. The audience comprises the Army top brass, Party bigwigs, city authorities and whoever else has somehow managed to lay claim to a seat. The musicians' frock coats are stuffed with newspapers, not because of the cold – although the past winter had already killed off thousands – but to fill them out in a way their famished bodies cannot. The rest of the audience, apart from the officials, have dressed up as best they can, and this might mean anything: hardened men have been seen wearing ladies' coats this winter, or endless layers of clothing in assorted colours. The conductor is Karl Eliasberg and he climbs onto the podium in rags. Three of his musicians have starved to death before they could even make the premiere. It is summer and it is cloudy; anyone who doesn't have access to a radio can go out and listen to the concert on the street corners, where loudspeakers have been hung. The summer is marked by an unbearable stench; the bodies can't be collected fast enough. They are piled up every few blocks, not before being thoroughly searched for anything that might be of value. Everything is valuable there in Leningrad, where the Germans have had the city surrounded for almost a year. Of the original orchestra only fifteen members remain, the rest decimated by hunger, bullets or the cold. Their replacements were recruited by whatever means possible. In fact, any musicians fighting on the front line were obliged to sign up for the orchestra.

The theatre is full. No admission has been charged as all the attendees are there by strict invitation, and those not invited can neither pay nor offer anything in exchange, apart from their unconditional loyalty to a cause that the concert organisers and musicians know is lost because the programme includes Bruckner's Symphony No. 5, the code and watchword for when there is nothing left to defend. Once the performance is over, audience members are offered a cyanide capsule – free of charge, naturally. The orchestra are dressed in immaculate suits. Indeed, everything is immaculate. Only three musicians have committed suicide. A bassoon, a double bass and a violin. All those in attendance occupy a state of certainty that only a triumph both unexpected and impossible can breach. In the streets, people sift through rubble in search of anything that might come in useful. Albert Speer has ordered that electricity be restored to Berlin for a few hours so the city philharmonic can perform a programme that includes, in addition to Bruckner, Beethoven's Violin Concerto and the end of Wagner's *Twilight of the Gods*, the scene of Brünnhilde's immolation. Outside the theatre, the women know it's a matter of days before they're raped by the nearly one million Russians who are just fifty kilometres away; their only hope is to seduce a high-ranking officer, and even then, who knows.

Shostakovich begins composing his Seventh Symphony in Leningrad. He wants to sign up for the front line, but the Party considers him too valuable and only allows him to serve as a firefighter, and it's in a fireman's helmet that he appears on the cover of *Time* in 1942 when his symphony crosses the Atlantic on microfilm and is performed in New York, conducted by Toscanini. In December, the authorities finally oblige him to flee the city with his family and head for Moscow.

The Germans choose not to make a final assault on Leningrad – they're not prepared to support a city of three million inhabitants in the event of victory – but rather to surround it and leave nature to do what it does best. And when nothing separates us from nature, a kind of slippage takes place. First the adults begin to behave like adolescents, then like children, and later like gods, until they reach the age of one year old, when there's no difference between walking and stumbling. So everyone is aged one here. But we're not all equal when it comes to hunger and cold; those who transcend their animal condition are the ones who save us in the end.

There are cries that don't seem human, piercing the Leningrad night, there are cries that aren't human in the nights that now surround Berlin, waiting for time to grant them their turn: the howls that come from the future sound like a muffled storm. In less than four days, the Russians are at the Brandenburg Gate. Three million babies in search of a lullaby, a scrap to quell their hunger, a bedtime story that will put them to sleep so they can stop thinking about those bodies piled in the street they'd cut the buttocks from in order to put something in their bellies. The snow hushes all sounds. Death steals the thickness from silence in the Leningrad winter, a silence that could sharpen knives in the Berlin night.

In March 1942 the Seventh Symphony has its premiere in Samara, the provisional capital of the USSR should Moscow fall. We are 1,700 kilometres southeast of

Leningrad, safe from everything, and it will be performed by the Bolshoi Theatre orchestra, conducted by Samuil Samosud. The symphony is triumphant from the get-go, as if it were already coming to an end, a kind of spell like the one fans cast when they yell *Goal!* before the player has taken the corner. Two minutes in, things calm down a little; a flute establishes a bit of order, as if appealing for patience. At one point a rather silly motif is heard that paraphrases the aria 'You'll Find Me at Maxim's' from the operetta *The Merry Widow*, one of Hitler's favourites. It's a march, with the snare drum keeping time, and, like in Ravel's *Bolero*, the intensity increases as the theme repeats. The theme of this section is 'invasion'. The climax is powerful and very low-pitched. Socialist realism brought to a crystalline state of perfection; this time the authorities don't demand the usual explanations from the composer, who has always kept one foot in Siberia after his decadent, bourgeois opera *Lady Macbeth*. Musicians are essential when death is imminent, and it is neither easy nor appropriate to ignore them. And if you're not convinced, take a look at the concentration camps: every barracks had someone who knew how to sing, a musician who could transport the prisoners back home. This happened to a Jewish man by the name of Svetliza who, before entering that endless loop of delirium known as Auschwitz, had been a well-known theatre impresario in Vienna. Svetliza was deeply moved when another prisoner sang a popular opera aria one night of heavy rain in the barracks. He asked the man if he knew any others. The prisoner did not, with the predictable exception of the melody to '*O sole mio*'. He sang quite well, mostly popular songs with easy melodies. He'd worked in cabarets, and one night claimed to have made a gramophone recording, though no one in the camp seemed to have heard of it. His name was Gleszer. Svetliza asked him to repeat the aria, which he pronounced phonetically, having learned it by ear. Of course, the man replied – in exchange for a piece of bread I'll sing whatever you like. No one has anything at all in a *Lager* at that time of night, but Svetliza promised to give him part of his next day's rations if he sang the song again. The man wouldn't be swayed. No bread, no music. Svetliza understands that it's better this way: now he has a reason to live until tomorrow.

On the long train journey to a prisoner–of–war camp in Silesia, Olivier Messiaen befriends a clarinettist by the name of Henri Akoka. Resigned to an uncertain future, they discuss different aspects of music. They talk of rhythms and tempo. The rhythms of Hindustan and Ancient Greece. The train carriage becomes a soundboard. One freezing night, the horror of the camp fades away. There's a green and purple curtain in the sky that furls and unfurls before the composer's astonished gaze. Most extraordinary of all is that the aurora borealis quite literally breaks the silence of the snow: Messiaen can hear it, just as he had heard with complete clarity the music that was carried by the sunlight through the stained glass windows of Sainte-Chapelle when he was a boy back in Paris. Northern lights made of glass. The synaesthesia was absolute: the music caused him to see colours, and the colours, music. Those colours spilling out over the frozen night sky mapped out, perhaps in its entirety, one of the greatest compositions of the twentieth century: the *Quartet for the End of Time*.

'I've seen a mighty angel coming down from heaven, wrapped in cloud, with a rainbow round his head. His face was like the sun, his feet like pillars of fire.' These are the lines from the Book of Revelations that Messiaen used as an epigraph for the score of the *Quartet*.

In the camp he met Carl-Albert Brüll, a guard who had been a lawyer before the war and who hated the Nazi regime. He got hold of paper and pencil for Messiaen and found ways of allowing him time to compose, exempting him from certain duties. The *Quartet* was written in the camp latrines. Clarinet, piano, violin and cello. A combination of timbres hardly typical of chamber music. Indeed, very little about the piece is typical, including the fact that there was no chance to rehearse, and the camp officers were sitting in the front row on the night of the first performance, in the perishing cold. And they applauded. All this happened in January 1941.

Messaien: The four musicians played on broken instruments... the keys on my upright piano stayed lowered when pressed... I played my quartet on this piano, with my three fellow musicians, dressed in the oddest way: in completely tattered clothes and wooden clogs large enough for the blood to circulate despite the snow underfoot.

Akoka: The audience, as far as I remember, was overwhelmed. They wondered what had happened. Everyone. Including us. We asked ourselves: 'What are we doing? What are we playing?'

The sole concession the quartet makes to untrained ears may be the final section, which is called 'Praise to the Immortality of Jesus'. It's a duet for violin and piano, and as it advances it becomes slower and higher, quieter and quieter. An almost infinite ascent. The eyes close as the ears open to capture a bird's final notes as it flies off into the depths of the night.

In the ridiculous military training we received prior to disembarking in the Falklands, we practised parading to the sound of patriotic marches. One day, the band played a couple of tunes to help the soldiers relax. Perhaps we'd paraded particularly well. I think they played the tango 'La cumparsita', which is based on a marching song, and something else, before performing 'When the Saints Go Marching In'. There's something deeply illogical about a military band playing jazz, an impossibility that lodges itself in each beat, because a military band doesn't breathe the instruments; it blows them, as if the promise of freedom offered by certain kinds of music knocked the wind out of it and left it gasping for air. But let's suppose the band played jazz. Suddenly one soldier, Zapata, is transformed. He begins to dance on the spot in a comical manner, as if walking in place. The faces he pulls are side-splittingly funny. The officers let him carry on. Everyone is laughing. Zapata was the hero that day in March 1982.

The Royal Palace of Madrid is home to the so-called Palatine Quartet, comprising two violins, a viola and a cello, all made by Stradivarius between 1696 and 1709.

The same day that the Battle of the Ebro marks a decisive turning point in the course of the Spanish Civil War, the Republican government in Madrid has these Stradivariuses brought out of the Royal Palace for the first time. The subsequent evening concert is broadcast across the country from the studios of the Propaganda and Press Ministry.

Franco's army bombards Madrid from Casa de Campo, like a heavyweight certain of landing the knockout blow. Every now and again a well-aimed punch threatens to topple what is left of the city. But on that September night in 1938, the strings have left the Palace. What for some is a requiem, for others is cause for celebration. All over Spain. The quartet of instruments is joined by another violin and a piano. They play Schubert, Bach, Rolla.

And once the concert is over, even though no one is chasing him, because it seems he was neither a Republican nor Nationalist and had never shown much interest in politics, the violist Pedro Meroño returns the instrument like someone returning a baby to its mother, bids farewell to the musicians with a firm handshake and heads into the street. As soon as he's around the first corner, he begins to run. First a gentle trot, and then, as his lungs grow used to the exertion, he picks up the pace until he's sprinting. Who's that lunatic, asks a man emerging into the street after hearing the performance; others may have seen him tear past their windows. To the gaze of those peering out, he appears as no more than a suspicious streak. He runs a couple more blocks without anyone coming after him. No one. He stops. He doubles over, his hands on his knees, staring at the ground. He bursts into tears. In the distance a dog barks, just like in any city in the world at this time of night.

What can I offer you to let me stay here a little longer, here in this room, listening to these cassettes that loosen the chest and allow the tears to flow of their own accord? Five minutes each, that was the agreement made there in the Falklands by a bunch of eighteen-year-old kids who had taken their end-of-school-year trips to Carlos Paz or Bariloche just six months before. What can I offer you, what's a minute of weeping worth on these shitty islands? There wasn't much to choose from, but it all served to carry you back, to your home, to your school, to those scruffy playing fields.

Did Zapata ever line up for his turn? After the war, I never heard of him again.

There was no way to pay for a ticket to that concert in Leningrad.

And in Berlin no one sings anymore, just as no one wants to say the word *Russians*.

The rump of even a rotting horse can still be saved, observes one of the musicians going into the rehearsal. So far, no cases of cannibalism have been reported. Yesterday the trumpet player barely had enough breath to blow with, the conductor noticed.

On the first movement of his Seventh, Shostakovich remarks many years later: 'The invasion theme has nothing to do with the attack. I was thinking about other enemies of humanity when I composed this section. I've nothing against calling the Seventh Symphony "Leningrad", but it's not about Leningrad under siege. It's about the Leningrad that Stalin destroyed and Hitler merely finished off.'

In one pocket, Svetliza keeps a little bread for the night. As the day goes by, the crust grows heavier and heavier, at a rate of one thousand kilos per hour (the body turns a shade of ochre at this point) and, when he hands it over to Gleszer and watches it disappear into the man's mouth in a joyless instant, his body is not at ease until the aria emerges from the same place the bread went, carrying him to the Vienna Opera House, and from there to eat with his wife and the actors at a mouth-watering delicatessen, and then further back, further down the years, when you were still in school, Zapata, discovering a rare talent and drawing pictures of soldiers crossing the Andes in those jotters whose covers you'd protect with spare wallpaper, while the clowns Gaby, Fofó and Miliki sang their ditty about the crazy hen and the radio was already playing that Creedence song, without you even knowing it, in the English of the enemy, which now speaks to you of returning to the dance where you dared to kiss a girl and climb onto the roof of your house, and also of the celebratory night from a prosperous time when the banknotes were counted by weight and the baritone Hans Hotter hugged you warmly behind the curtain after that luminous aria that now languishes in the mouth of someone who will demand another mouthful if you want to return to Vienna the next day, as all the inhabitants of Leningrad return to Leningrad when the zombie orchestra of gasping trumpet players begins to play the Seventh Symphony, which sounds better than if the Berlin Philharmonic were playing it, even for the Germans on the outskirts of the city who recognise the march coming over the loudspeakers in the streets as the insipid little tune from *The Merry Widow* and suddenly wonder where they are, and who are their enemies. Yes, like tired horses trotting home, something weightless floats away from the listening bodies and returns to that place where no songs or arias or orchestras are needed. They're banging on the door, your five minutes of weeping are up. Better find more bread for tomorrow.

That night Svetliza delivers the bread to Gleszer. He's scraped at the crust, gaining a few crumbs, and nibbled at the end concealed in his hand. He's bitten it as if it were his first kiss, with all his desire and fear marching in step (never again: either save it or eat it, and that's that). It's lucky that Gleszer doesn't bother examining his payment before he devours it in three swift mouthfuls. Svetliza lowers his head, not wanting to witness the ceremony of his fasting in another man's throat. The prisoner sings and for some reason does so with greater gusto than usual, making an effort to pronounce the most difficult parts. Svetliza raises his head again and looks to one side, to the left. He weeps gently, tearless.

People crowd around the loudspeakers on the streets of Leningrad. Some listen on the radio; others stay in their houses, hovering by the windows. There hasn't been a single unbroken pane in the city for a year. In winter the gaps are covered with whatever's to hand and the houses become cold, dark caves, but for now, with the windows open, the music enters and will stay, in the crumbling, mouldy walls, for as many winters as it takes.

In his memoir published after the war, Albert Speer himself reflected that including *The Twilight of the Gods* in the programme had been a melancholy gesture, even a pathetic one. As if all the rest of the Nazi iconography and aesthetic were not. All those decorated wagons in the patriotic parades as if the end of the world, the Ragnarök, belonged in the pages of the *Popul Vuh* or some equally exotic sacred book. How could they ever win a war like that.

For some reason or for none at all, because in the camps people are punished or killed without reason every day, the prisoners have spent almost the whole night lined up without moving in the cold. After three hours half a dozen are lying dead. Svetliza is very weak; Gleszer has demanded payment in advance this evening.

One more hour, three new bodies in the snow. The guards break up the lines without saying why. Back in the bunks, Gleszer approaches Svetliza. I'm not forgetting you've paid already, he says, but let's leave it until tomorrow, please. Svetliza concurs. No one has strength for anything. The prisoner is a man of his word and respects the laws of the market; the next evening he sings the aria again. Svetliza has eaten his bread and this is the only time he hears it with anything in his stomach.

Gleszer is sitting on his bunk waiting for Svetliza. He is growing impatient; he's hungry and wants his extra piece of bread. He turns his head towards the sector where his patron sleeps. No one moves; it seems that no one is awake. Does anyone else pay him to sing? We don't know; perhaps he only demands payment for very specific requests. He lies down without asking himself any further questions.

The next day someone tells him Svetliza is in hospital. He received a blow from a rifle butt the previous evening, he's very weak, he's got typhus, who knows. Anything could have landed him there, to be honest.

Only late on will Messiaen notice a major omission in the performance of his *Quartet*. Perhaps this well-earned guilt is the reason why – despite Brüll having helped him escape along with three other musicians (and many more people, we now know) – he refuses to receive the former camp guard when he comes to visit him in Paris after the war.

Messiaen was a Catholic with mystical leanings, open

to more contemplative types of wisdom. However, he was incapable of putting himself in the place of the other prisoners for even a moment and play something after the concert – or even beforehand – that would carry them back to the warmth of the good earth. Something familiar they could hum. *Give us something to clap along to, Messiaen!* It's not easy to keep up with the melodies and the tempo amidst all that avant-garde business. He only thinks about his music. And that sounds like salvation for just one man (though no one can be judged for doing these things in a prisoner-of-war camp). That's why he was exaggerating the time he claimed he had never been listened to with such devotion.

Perhaps he realised his omission when he heard the story of Herbert Zipper, a composer and orchestra conductor who was freed from the Dachau concentration camp before the war began. Zipper started by reciting poems to the prisoners. Everyone stopped to listen; it meant some kind of return to normality, even if none of them had ever had a poem recited to them in their former lives. This was how he met a poet, Jura Soyfer, with whom he composed the 'Dachau Lied', a song with a martial rhythm that, like a virus, reached all the camps. It was deliberately difficult to learn because Zipper's intention, he later recalled, was that the prisoners should make an effort to rise above their circumstances. This ruse had occurred to him when he was forced for days to push, pointlessly, Sisyphus-style, a barrow-load of cement.

Keep step, comrade. Head up, comrade, and think always of the day the bells of freedom will ring.

In the camp, Zipper met some musicians and encouraged the ones assigned carpentry tasks to build instruments with what wood they were able to steal. In this way they formed an orchestra that played in the camp latrine on Sunday afternoons, when many of the guards had leave. They performed classic works that all or most of them already knew, together with pieces composed especially for them by Zipper.

A week has gone by since the last time he sang. This evening the prisoners have formed lines three deep. Gleszer is in the second row. He's heard they're going to be taken off to repair roofs. For over an hour they've been waiting for who knows what. Two guards talk and laugh. A third arrives with a sheet of paper. One of them reads it and waves his hand towards some distant point, while the other shrugs and keeps laughing. Suddenly a procession of bodies appears from the left, robbed of all vitality, little but skin and bones. Glezser spots Svetliza marching among them. He's bent over and limping; he's shat himself. And so Glezser begins singing soundlessly, his mouth wide open as if he were yawning. The guards don't even notice. At that moment Svetliza raises his head and it seems as if he's going to turn his head towards the group, but no, it falls again, swaying from side to side, affirming and denying at the same time. Convulsive movements like eyes in a decapitated head. Glezser opens his mouth a little wider and watches as before him and behind him everyone lined up sings that marvellous aria without voice and without bread; their pronunciation is perfect because they sing it in all the languages of the world at once. Can't Svetliza hear the aria? Glezser puffs out his chest and things change: something straightens his friend's back a little and he adjusts his frock coat as the audience enters the theatre, another exceptional gala performance that will end, as always, with everyone singing the 'Drinking Song' from *La Traviata*, well into the night in the finest restaurant in Vienna. Svetliza stumbles with the joyful wine of a glorious evening, because the prisoner behind him utters a rasping sound and clutches at his striped pyjamas so as not to fall into the mud. A guard approaches and Glezser leaves off singing. Everyone stops at once. He stares at the ground and doesn't see Svetliza disappearing into a black hole.

That night, Glezser sings the aria for everyone in the barracks.

At the end of the *Twilight of the Gods*, following Brünnhilde's immolation and the overflowing of the Rhine, when Valhalla is in flames and all the gods are burning together in the fire, Odin going down last of all – when all has been consumed, a light fanfare is heard, as if someone were returning, exhausted, to the gentle earth. At that moment, there emerges a valley emptied of gods, nature freed of all will.

Strident clapping in Berlin, like rainfall, like a retreating parade, in unison, like hooves disappearing into the distance. No one asks for an encore. After that concert, where is there left to go?

In Leningrad the end of the symphony is received at first with silence.

'And suddenly a storm of applause broke out,' recalls Ksenia Matus.

And a little girl carries a bouquet of red flowers to the conductor. It was the only touch of colour in a world without people, without gods, just children who wait for the night to pass (and if there are flowers, it's because the black fog is going to clear).

More hunger will come, and more cold and more death. But there are red flowers. This is food for the eyes. Knowing this, every morning will be a child from now on.

And every night a womb.
With such knowledge, no one can lose a war.

SKY ANTS

Didgeridoo is the Western name for a musical instrument used by the Aboriginal peoples of northern Australia, a region known to them as Yidaki. It is made from a eucalyptus trunk hollowed out by termites that produces a nocturnal sound when beeswax is applied to the mouthpiece, a black wind, something thick and slow, unstoppable. It also resembles those earliest electric pedals used in rock music, which sound old today because of just how modern they were then.

In the dreamtime, Bur Buk Boon was carrying firewood to his family because it was a frigid night. When he tossed his pile of branches to the ground, he noticed that one was hollow and full of ants. Masses of ants. He raised it up and blew hard on one end to expel them. The ants climbed into the sky and became the stars.

If we bring our ear to a didgeridoo, we can hear Bur Buk Boon blowing through it.

The sound of the night shut up in a tree.

Almost like locking up an earthquake.

The didgeridoo has a unique characteristic: a circular sound can be achieved by building up air in the mouth, then inhaling through the nose at the same time as blowing, and then, while continuing to exhale, blocking the glottis and letting out the air retained in the cheeks. It seems impossible, but it comes with practice.

When does a concert performed with this instrument end?

Music is continuous, it is only attention that falters, wrote Thoreau.

The distance between the planets is proportional to the distance between musical notes, Pythagoras reasoned. And since the sounds they emit as they move never stop, we can never truly hear the music of the spheres. Their constancy leaves us deaf to them, like the sound of the sea to a fisherman. The cosmic order is a musical order. Kepler also understood it this way, as asserted in his 1619 treatise *Harmonices Mundi*: 'The heavenly motions are nothing but a continuous song for several voices, to be perceived by the intellect, not by the ear; a music which, through discordant tensions, through syncopations and cadenzas as it were, progresses toward certain predesigned six-voiced cadences, and thereby sets landmarks in the immeasurable flow of time.' The faster the movement, he added, and the closer to the sun a heavenly body travelled, the higher the note. And so he wrote six melodies, one for each planet.

The stars have internal vibrations that are something like an earthquake. They generate sound waves that deform the surface. The frequency of these waves is around 3,000 Hz. We can't hear them directly as they cannot travel across space, but we can use a helioseismograph to observe how they deform its surface. Tsunamis of fire across the sun. These frequencies have been converted into audible sounds for us to hear. They sound remarkably like the song of the loneliest whale in the world.

Between 1645 and 1715 the sunspots disappeared from the sun. This phenomenon caused a series of harsh winters. Fir trees, pines and maples grew as straight and firm as Cossacks. As a result, their wood acquired a rare temper. About this time, Antonio Stradivari was making his famous violins and cellos. Researchers have discovered that these climatic conditions are key to understanding their exceptional sound. That's not the whole explanation, of course: not all instruments from the same period sound quite so extraordinary. Yet in no sense does this undermine the music that comes from space.

When the solar wind collides with the Earth's magnetic field, it gives rise to the aurora borealis.

In 1977, the *Voyager* probe headed into space, carrying a golden disc of sounds from Earth, including greetings in almost sixty languages and a range of folk and cultivated music from many cultures. The third track involves a didgeridoo. It contains, in fact, two early songs from Australia: one is called 'Morning Star' and the other 'Devil Bird'. The first is associated with a ritual to accompany the soul of the deceased on its journey to a star.

Another track on the golden record is the 'Prelude and Fugue in C Major' from the Second Book of the *Well-Tempered Clavier*, performed by Glenn Gould.

According to the calculations, in the remote chance that another civilization hears the record, at least 40,000 years would have passed.

Forty thousand years ago, no human being had set foot on the American continent. Hairy rhinoceros, megatheria and sabre-toothed tigers roamed the land. And there was music too. The oldest musical instrument on record is a little flute that Neanderthal man fashioned from a swan's femur. It was found in Germany and is

43,000 years old; there must be older examples, as it already looks well-evolved.

It isn't hard to imagine that the flute's origin lay in a piece of bone or hollow wood instinctively raised to the lips to blow through. Perhaps someone found such a piece with a natural hole on the upper surface? Placing a finger to the hole, the change in sound is apparent. The true revolution lies in the second hole. Making a nothingness.

Voyager's message is aimed at inhabitants not of other worlds, but of our own.

Hearing from time to time that the probe has left behind

the asteroid belt

the rings of Saturn

the solar system

the heliopause, where the solar wind dies away and the wind from other stars begins to be felt

the Milky Way.

Ever further

in space and time.

Every now and again the newspapers report on its distance and replay the greetings in all the different languages and tell us about the music out there,

further and further away from us

so that we can be closer to one another.

At some point *Voyager* will run into the galaxy formed by the ants of the Australian Aboriginals.

A celestial anthill of white ants.

Following a debate conducted with the violent cordiality of people who have known each other for a long time, the five candidates for mayor of Bahía Blanca were asked about their musical preferences. It was the only moment of the night that everyone smiled. This happened in 2015.

The EMI record label, owner of the Beatles' rights, refused to let the song 'Here Comes the Sun' be added to the journey of the *Voyager*.

The brain of each ant contains a miniscule cell of a collective brain, which has no specific place in space, only in time. The anthill isn't a collection of individuals but one great mind that organises tasks and structures for its survival. No ant laments the death of another ant. Multinational companies are not much different.

It's impossible to be sure how many ants there are in the world, or how many anthills; generous calculations have been ventured, but nothing very serious.

What's more certain is that there are between one hundred and three hundred thousand trillion stars in the sky.

The number of neurons in a human brain is similar to the number of stars in a galaxy: between one hundred and two hundred thousand million.

The stars are the neurons of the galaxies.

And the galaxies, brains roaming the cosmos, singing songs we cannot hear.

Voyager also carries whale songs.

The disc begins with a work by the composer Laurie Spiegel based on Kepler's *Harmonices Mundi*. Keyboards and choirs. Nothing out of this world, really.

Our galaxy knows that we've sent a rocket filled with messages into space, just like every anthill knows about a missing ant.

The Milky Way cannot communicate with us because a brain doesn't communicate with a neuron; the anthill doesn't communicate with the ant. And a mere planet is barely even a neuron.

We are a part of its thought process.

Other worlds might find the *Voyager* spacecraft and realise that we are the lost ant.

For unless you are lost, you have no reason to go round asking questions out there in space.

The ant knows about the anthill.

The only way they can possibly respond is: don't send any more rockets.

We'll destroy them.

Could a similar disc not have passed close to the Earth once, a lost ant we failed to notice, busy as we were building didgeridoos?

Messiaen in the forests of France, transcribing birdsong into musical notation.

More than 40,000 years separate us from a score we are unable to read.

EXOTIC BIRDS

 It can only be a relief that death took Scriabin before he was able to complete his *Mysterium*, with which he intended to destroy the world and thus make way for a new humanity. It seems this new humanity would be drawn from among the hypothetical attendees of a single concert performed in the foothills of the Himalayas, in a circular church at whose centre a pool of water would invert the sky. The ceremony was to go on for seven days and seven nights. A demented performance. A work that was going to do away with all works of art and fling open the doors of perception once and for all. For *Mysterium* was a musical work that would also include perfumes, textures, coloured lights emerging from an organ, words, choreographies, fire, gazes, dances, smoke, columns of incense, fog that would alter the outline of the cathedral, caresses. The audience weren't meant to keep still. Dressed in regulation white, they all had to participate in some way: either playing an instrument or dancing or walking in procession. A mass for the end of days. The work expanded in his mind, but not on the score. Over twelve years, from 1903 until his death, the idea was like a woodpecker in his head. All he left behind on paper was a kind of study, a prelude entitled the 'Preliminary Action' which would ready the musicians and audience alike for performing the *Mysterium*. A warm-up of sorts.

In his papers, and in his exchanges with his wife and confidante, everything grew more and more spectacular, and thus incomprehensible. The idea was to provoke an overwhelming ecstasy of all individual forms. It was meant to begin with a pealing of bells hung from the clouds themselves. Scriabin's enthusiasm expanded in line with his delirium: he went as far as to buy a plot of land in India where he planned to put the idea into action. But if we should see Ligeti's *Symphonic Poem for 100 Metronomes* as an installation, then *Mysterium* is conceptual music or, if we like, one of those children's games focused on enumerating rules and obstacles that never actually gets played. The point of toy soldiers, for example, was always to set the stage, arrange the armies, prepare deployments, but never to actually engage in battle, just as it was never the point to elucidate a method of determining the winner of a game only destined to be interrupted by snack time, by the doorbell ringing, by anything at all. Sometimes things present themselves in their roughest form, uncut and unpolished, when they could develop in countless ways; there is something prior to a story that only preserves its meaning if it advances towards all its potential unfoldings simultaneously. We find it in the story of the only two survivors of the Second World War who knew the locations of the three separate parts into which the original score of Beethoven's Symphony No. 9 had been divided to protect it from bombs and looting. Neither knew the other's fate; one fragment of the manuscript had been left in the Russian sector of Berlin, the other two in the sector controlled by the Yanks. It's also there in the story of Bill Millin, personal piper to Lord Lovat, an eccentric yet brilliant Scottish commander who disembarked on the beaches at Normandy ('This is going to be the greatest invasion in history and I want the bagpipes leading it'), and whom the German snipers didn't bother firing at because they didn't want to waste bullets on a madman. Are these not veritable Schrödinger's cats, neither dead nor alive until we leave them alone – the sadness of María Sabina, the shaman of Oaxaca whose songs were stolen and recorded on tape? Isn't it another cat poised in a 'let's see', her hopeless surprise at the sound of her own voice played back? Or the story of Jimmie Nicol, the man who was a Beatle for ten days in 1964, replacing Ringo on tour. That's a punishment dreamt up by Olympian gods right there. How many bells hang from the clouds in the skies over Bayreuth, or in the concerts for bell towers of the Catalan composer Llorenç Barber? A marble block awaiting the chisel: this is the *Beethoven's Tenth Symphony* composed by Leandro Monasterio by overlaying its nine forerunners to form a thick soup; fragments of each can be picked out of what sounds like a traffic jam on the verge of explosion; everything is about to end at any moment; it's the very sound of imminence (how long can we go on listening to something like this?). And this tenth symphony, doesn't it become unnecessary? Should we superimpose, for example, the two wedding marches written by Mendelssohn, a Jew, and the anti-Semite Wagner, respectively? Neither dead nor alive, that cat, even when we learn that Bill Millin played the bagpipes again at the funeral – fifty-three years later – of his former commander.

Tolstoy twice invited Scriabin to play the piano at his residence in Yasnaya Polyana. He found the composer's music to be pleasant and sincere. He also invited Wanda Landowska, the greatest harpsichord player of the twentieth century, who studied the *Goldberg Variations* for over forty-five years – almost the same amount of time that Glenn Gould was alive. Tolstoy wasn't well enough to travel to Moscow to hear her play. Landowska, who felt a bulletproof admiration for him, was dying to meet the writer. She visited him twice in 1909, first in January and again in December. Only on the second visit did anything happen to interest Tolstoy, who was always universally bored ('her flattery is disagreeable', he wrote in his diary), and he had not been impressed by the music he had heard.

Two days before New Year, Landowska and her husband are travelling by horse-drawn sleigh to the writer's residence. The harpsichord is strapped to the back. It's bitterly cold. Compelled by one of those reasons only the body understands, the driver comes to a halt; something's not right with the sleigh, or at least not the same as it was a moment ago. He checks and, yes, the harpsichord has disappeared. It's getting late, and the snow has been falling steadily for a while now. Landowska tries to keep calm, but her husband has the bright idea of telling her what he should have mentioned much earlier: he thought he'd heard the sound of something falling, but it never occurred to him it could be the instrument. It really never crossed my mind, he'll tell Tolstoy later that night. Meanwhile, anger and tears from his wife. The sleigh driver makes an about-turn and they head back in search of the harpsichord. They have to hurry; their tracks are quickly being filled in. After longer than seems wise, the sled halts again. The best thing would be for the two men to search the area. It can't be far. Landowska doesn't comply with the suggestion to remain with the sleigh and follows in her husband's steps, or at least in the direction she thinks he's gone. She advances through the snow, her tears propelling her onwards. The cold turns the air to mist and the sky draws nearer, the colours merge, the sounds separate out. She is lost. She shouts, but fear breaks her voice. She walks on a little further and suddenly there it is, the harpsichord, in a little hollow. She runs towards it as if it were a lost child. She rights it and checks it over for damage. She tries to shout again but all that comes out is a low moan. Instead, she opens the lid of the harpsichord and bangs on the keys to call the men's attention. But such a sound could be confused with a flock of birds taking flight. She calms herself, takes off her gloves and begins to play. The same tune over and over. The first to hear the melody is the sleigh driver; he struggles through the snow to the harpsichord. He comes to a halt before he reaches it, on the brink of the abyss. He can't interrupt her because he's six years old again and doesn't know if he even feels the cold any longer. Perhaps he does, but it doesn't matter: it's always good to feel a bit cold when your parents are nearby. And so he remains until the husband's cry wraps itself around Landowska; more than fifty years pass in an instant. Let's go, come on, he says when he reaches them, it's dangerous for us to stay here. Tolstoy wants to know what she was playing, but his guest can't really remember. Bach, she thinks, or perhaps Scarlatti, repeating it over and over to form a great circle.

That night, Landowska performs a few of the *Goldberg Variations*. Count Tolstoy seems deep in concentration, his head resting on his hand, but in fact he is making an extraordinary effort to stay awake, his wife Sofia notes. He shakes off his drowsiness when, in advance of the arrival of some delicious pastries, his guest plays a silly little ditty, 'Old Man Dance', a favourite of Tolstoy's. He asks her to play it three times in a row. And then again. He is wide awake now.

Of her host's books Landowska prefers – needless to say – *The Kreutzer Sonata*, but as soon as she tries to discuss it, Tolstoy changes the subject. Published in 1889, the novel had become a kind of premonition. In summary, the protagonist learns that his wife is having an affair with a musician with whom she practices the sonata in question. He becomes enraged with jealousy and eventually he kills her. A striking plot that expresses the author's ideas on love, chastity, matrimony. And just a few years later, the pianist and composer Sergei Taneyev spends two summers in Tolstoy's residence. Sofia falls madly in love; her behaviour becomes disconcerting and infuriating, childish in a way that sends Tolstoy into a jealous fit. He writes in his diary that the visiting musician is the embodiment of stupidity. He knows his wife will go no further than flirting with him, but it annoys him in the extreme that he has stooped to feeling jealousy, as though his wife were a possession. Sofia has even decided to learn to play the piano properly, with a female tutor recommended by Taneyev, and muses aloud on her idea of a concert for four hands. She takes a lot of photographs of him (this was an art of great interest to her, and she had taken dozens of Tolstoy, bringing out his involuntary air of a biblical patriarch). Nevertheless, the novel does not turn out to be premonitory after all. The explanation is banal, and therefore hard to believe. The woman has decided, as fed up of her husband as she is in love with him, to complete the storyline. As if it were a score to perform. In the first few pages of the book, the protagonist − clearly the voice of the author − says the following about love: 'In life, this preference for one person above everyone else can last maybe for some years, but that's very rare. Much more often it lasts for only a few months, or weeks, or days, or hours even.' Her love will last much more than a few months. Just to give you an idea: three times over she copied out by hand *War and Peace*, which comes in at more than a thousand pages. (Alma Mahler did something similar with her husband's scores, though she also cheated on him with the architect Walter Gropius.)

Sofia had taken the photograph showing Landowska and Tolstoy together. This is one of the few belongings the harpsichordist manages to take with her when the Nazis invade France, leaving behind her library of over ten thousand volumes and her collection of antique instruments. The flight is chaotic. She had recorded Scarlatti's harpsichord sonatas on that very same day. The German artillery can clearly be heard in the recording. Such is Landowska's concentration that she doesn't miss a beat. It is fortunate that the sound engineers weren't able to erase the explosions in the background: today they may be more valuable than the rest. Nor could they cut out the cries of *Viva Italia!* when Maria Callas recorded *Va pensiero* in the San Carlo theatre in Naples, as the end of the Second World War was declared. The exact opposite of what happened when Johnny Cash recorded his performance of *Folsom Prison Blues* in 1968: the applause and cries of the inmates had to be added later on, to give the impression of a live concert. Devoted silence for the musician who sings 'I shot a man in Reno, just to watch him die.' A year earlier, the Beatles opened *Sgt. Pepper's* with the sounds of a concert. Wild applause.

Before it went on sale, Landowska had access to Glenn Gould's first recording of the *Goldberg Variations*. She was fascinated with it. She had twice made recordings of her own: the first in 1933, the second in 1945. Or in other words, the years of the rise and fall of Hitler.

And the photo of the Russian giant, always there on her desk.

Taneyev died in 1915 from pneumonia contracted at the funeral of Scriabin, who had been his student.

The man who destroyed guitars when no one had a bloody amp heard the music of the spheres for the first time at the age of eleven while playing the harmonica in the drizzling rain after a failed fly-fishing trip. From that moment on, music becomes his inseparable ally in the fight that alcohol would later join as a reinforcement, for what happens the next day brings back to him the awful nights spent in his grandmother's house as a child. This is how Pete Townshend tells the story in his memoirs:

Suddenly I was hearing music inside the music – rich, complex harmonic beauty that had been locked in the sounds I'd been making.

And the next day:

...this time the murmuring sound of the river opened up a wellspring of music so enormous that I fell in and out of a trance.

Some time later, encouraged by a friend, he wants to sign up for the Sea Scouts.

I began to hear the most extraordinary music, sparked by the whine of the outboard motor and the burbling sound of water against the hull. I heard violins, cellos, horns, harps and voices, which increased in number until I could hear countless threads of an angelic choir.

When the music ceases, the child Pete begins to weep disconsolately, asking the other boys if they'd heard what he had.

Part of the initiation into the Sea Scouts is a cold shower. It's cold anyway, it's night-time, there's barely a lit bulb in a cubicle neither indoors nor outdoors, a shower against the mouldy wall, two Sea Scout captains laugh and jerk off while he trembles. Child Pete can't leave the shower until they're done. Then they chuck a towel his way.

A little over ten years later, Pete Townshend becomes not only one of the greatest rock music composers but the one who best understands the physicality of this music. A performer with a truly volcanic energy who never rehearsed his movements on stage. More than once, amid the electronic distortion, he could hear a music that no one was playing at that moment, coming from everywhere at once. The young Pete had composed a long song divided into six parts that caused a radical transformation in him when he played it at concerts: 'A Quick One, While He's Away' was a veritable catharsis of his past as an abused child. He would become enraged, he confesses in his memoirs, when at the end of the song, he yelled over and over the chorus line *You are forgiven*, and it was his grandmother and his parents and all their lovers and he himself who were forgiven.

And this music fell from the child's sky.

And there are vibrations that come to him in the middle of the concerts: 'They were becoming so pure that I thought the whole world was just going to stop, the whole thing was just becoming so unified.'

In the early 1970s, he is struck by an idea as powerful as it is inexpressible. The little he is able to understand involves a concert where the spectators would somehow feed the data that defines them as individuals into a synthesizer that would instantly transform it into sound patterns.

Tsunamis of the sun in translation. The sum of these harmonic sequences would produce a universal chord, he intuited. Whatever that might be.

Bells hanging from the clouds.

Hours of music were recorded in endless loops. The influence of Terry Riley, a pioneer of minimalism who more than once held concerts in the Rothko Chapel, is clear and present. The whole project, called *Lifehouse*, culminated in a great record, *Who's Next*, which turned out nothing like that mountain range of spiritual quavers imagined by the little boy who the night-time voices never allowed to fully grow up.

Messiaen: One of the great dramas of my life consists of my telling people that I see colours whenever I hear music, and they see nothing, nothing at all. That's terrible. And they don't even believe me. When I hear music, I see colours. Chords are expressed in terms of colour for me. I'm convinced that one can convey this to the listening public.

In spring, just before dawn, Oliver Messiaen would head out into the woods to hear the first birds of the day. He carried only his omnipresent satchel, full of papers and scores. He would transcribe the birdsong onto the stave: the best music in the world, he would say to anyone who would listen. He became an expert ornithologist. From these annotations, significant works emerged, such as *The Awakening of the Birds*. An unpredictable music that feels like it might end at any moment. There is something of conceptual art about it: told beforehand that it's about birds, the ear prepares itself for trilling and chirping, or something of the kind. The unpredictable not governed by chance: this is how birds sing and fly and move their heads. We have no idea what's coming, nor do we really remember what we've just heard. A pure music, animal, present.

Messiaen: Birds are the opposite to Time; they are our desire for light, for stars, for rainbows, and for jubilant songs. Each bird, each instrument has its own tempo, and by overlaying them we achieve a confused and joyous harmony.

Something like that universal chord?

Music to do away with the world, or time, which amounts to more or less the same thing.

In winter, when he travelled to the forests of Bellême to hear blackbirds, thrushes and nightingales, Messiaen would get up very early, long before dawn. What bird sings at that hour? His wife would hear him preparing coffee, which he always drank strong, and sometimes a thick soup, before he went out. She didn't accompany him on those freezing excursions. In fact, his mind wasn't set on hearing birds, but on catching an aurora borealis. Can they really be seen, so far south? asks his wife. Well, Silesia is at almost the same latitude as Bellême, a little further north but not much. Why should the auroras not reach this far?

He never saw another one. He remained in silence, watching the frozen sky in the forest clearings, until the first larks and cardinals arrived.

Yet are they not a kind of aurora borealis too, those great flocks that form complex figures as they move in overlapping planes? We don't see them in colour because we can hear their song.

The flock as one great flying brain.

Galaxy of Australian ants.

Then, when he was commissioned by the New York Chamber Music Society to compose a piece for the bicentenary of US independence, it didn't cross Messiaen's mind to go to the Big Apple to see the lights that had inspired the most musical of Mondrian's paintings. Instead he asked to travel to the Bryce Canyon in Utah, in order to contemplate a veritable aurora borealis in stone, which is also a kind of spirited Rothko, deep red and yellow in disordered, vivid strips. From this experience he composed *From the Canyons to the Stars*, another work made of pure present.

The sixth movement consists of a trumpet solo and a lot of silence.

It is titled 'Interstellar Call'.

Messiaen: The calls gradually become hoarser and more poignant: there is no answer! The calls are met by silence. In this silence there may be a response, which is worship.

He worked on the piece for three years and completed it in 1974. That year, the first radio signal was transmitted from the base in Arecibo, intended to be picked up by extra-terrestrial intelligence. It will take 25,000 years to reach its destination, the constellation of Hercules. We'll have to wait the same amount of time for a response.

Until at least early 1992, tourists or pilgrims arriving at the Church of the Holy Trinity in Paris could hear a music that sometimes, to an unsuspecting ear, sounded dissonant, or even as if a crack were opening up to let in the sky. Emerging from its complex rhythm were occasional traces of music hall, something by Gershwin, unpredictable melodies, oriental cadences. A miracle that the church would allow all this in its liturgy.

The organ certainly sounds strange. Nevertheless, Father Yves acknowledges that his words 'come to life' in mass whenever the organist improvises.

What's happened is that Messiaen has brought the aurora borealis back with him.

The artist Piet Mondrian and boogie-woogie arrive in New York and leave it again at almost the same time. The one from Holland, by way of London, fleeing the Nazis despite always sporting (seriously) a moustache just like the Führer's. The other from Kansas, by way of Chicago, brought by a Carnegie Hall producer in a memorable concert sponsored by the communist newspaper *New Masses*. Within a week the pianists involved were already cutting their gramophone records and filling the bars of Greenwich Village every night, especially the Café Society Downtown, which was fundraising for the communist cause. This was 1940.

Mondrian's strict Calvinist upbringing is in evidence in the austerity of his canvases: he reduces the colours to the three primaries, enclosing them in squares delineated by perfect black strips. Art as a way of life: he had nothing green in his home, and he turned corners at right angles. Honestly. And if his paintings say nothing, it is because that is precisely their purpose, to hush all emotion, all sentimentality. Their purpose, he wrote many times, is to crystallize the basic structure of reality. To go beyond appearances, drop the veil of Isis. He tired of explaining that his works were not purely formalist exercises but an attempt to reconcile polar opposites: the masculine and the feminine, for example, that he saw in horizontal and vertical lines. Veritable mandalas, his works.

Ethology is the study of animal behaviour, that is, what we see when we observe a dog. With the lenses of biology we can focus on its digestive system; chemistry allows us to zoom in on amino acids and sugars; if we wish to account for the molecules that make up the cells and the atoms that make up the molecules, we must turn to physics; and if our aim is to go beyond physics, beyond even the realm of leptons and quarks, then we shouldn't open a book by Leibniz or any other philosopher to see what there is on the other side, but enter a room where a Mondrian is hanging on the wall, and rest our gaze on the peace of his planes, focus on the junction of two black strips, for example, and wait for a cloud of galaxies to appear and then merge, as they approach, into one where we distinguish the star orbited by the planet whose bright blue becomes studded with green and brown patches as we move closer until, on the threshold of the eye, a city emerges in which we recognise in the yard of a suburban house a dog tired of barking at the only thing that dogs can see in colour.

Mondrian was always interested in music. In Amsterdam he had defended the explorations of one of the first minimalist composers, Jakob van Domselaer, and when the government prohibited public dances in 1915, there was no private party not invigorated by his personal dance style. He discovered jazz when he arrived in Paris and it sent him absolutely wild. He found in jazz the rhythm he needed for his painting and, when the rumour arrived that the Charleston would be prohibited in Holland as indecent, he lamented that he would never be able to return to his home country. Always seen in suit and tie, formal to the point of exhaustion, in great demand with women and incorrigibly penniless: swift but necessary biographical brushstrokes. He and the artist Lee Krasner – one of the most important of the post-war period – would go to dance to jazz at Minton's Playhouse, though nothing ever happened between them, as far as we know. He may have been in love.

The same evening he arrived in New York, he went to a bar to dance boogie until six in the morning. We are very fortunate that Mondrian's moves were never recorded on film. It is better to leave these things to the imagination, to visualise a stylish, graceful dancer and not some clumsy amateur. Something like this happened with the sole recording ever made of a castrato, the very last of them all, who has decidedly not taken his voice from the angels, despite having been a soloist in the Sistine Chapel choir for fifteen years; although we may concede there is something cherubic about his chubby face. His name is Alessandro Moreschi. He was born in 1858 and once he retired from singing he conducted the Vatican choir until 1913. The recordings are from 1905. Moreschi lacks both vocal technique and education. Recordings can be found on the internet of him performing Gounod's *Ave Maria*, and the effect is sinister, to say the least. Let's just say that a countertenor (the highest a male singer can reach) can be a little tiresome, just like the falsetto of certain rock singers. Moreschi sounds like a lamb on its way to the slaughter, all the more so if we observe one of the two photographs available online. We are beholding a totality, and this taxes our soul. The singer is not a man and a woman at one and the same time, but something altogether more complete: a man and a girl in a single body. A voice of contained hysteria and a gaze that in his portrait is held on the brink of smiling or of weeping, as if he knew our most intimate secret. That he died alone and in poverty is obvious from such a portrait.

Jazz and boogie deafen visitors to Mondrian's New York studio. The errant Dutchman is never still – indeed, in photos taken of him in this space, he is always slightly blurred. Mondrian is Dr Jekyll and Mr Hyde. He engenders a geometry of the severest Calvinism while off-canvas boogie echoes around the studio.

Unlike European cities, the streets of New York form a near-perfect grid animated by car lights, traffic lights and advertisements with flat, bright colours. In a city like this there is no need to turn the corner at a right angle, and one may dare to wear a green tie. And so the black strips are taken over by little squares of syncopated colour, like in jazz. And each of them obeys an irrefutable rhythmic logic. He spent a year that way, painting what is perhaps his masterpiece: *Broadway Boogie-Woogie*.

Piet Mondrian died in 1944 at the age of seventy-two, the same year that boogie fell out of fashion in New York. He left his painting *Victory Boogie-Woogie* unfinished.

Broadway is the only avenue that upsets the symmetry of Manhattan.

In 1945 Lee Krasner marries Jackson Pollock.

When the sun has almost set, and is barely a dish balancing on the horizon, flocks of birds are often seen flying high in the sky. They disappear in silence towards the last refuges of the light. Someone with acute vision can follow them for up to a minute, but even a momentary distraction makes it almost impossible to catch sight of them again. Something similar happens with music, with ninety percent of all compositions. Songs languish slowly until, one day, someone hears them whole for the last time. They survive in a chance whistled melody, in the phrasing of a jazz piano, in an advert. Relentlessly, they fray away to nothing. Some lodge themselves in our heads for days in the form of a few beats before they devolve into something like Chinese water torture.

Often what began as an indolent riff turns into an insufferable mantra that the band is forced to play at some point in the concert if they don't want the audience to set fire to the theatre. It's important to think very hard about what bedtime stories to tell children, as grandmothers well know. There's not much difference between Sisyphus, a story before bed and a hit song. Musicians and grandmothers alike know that the story doesn't belong to them, that they have to sing and that's that; perhaps there's room for a little embellishment, through gritted teeth, like the pinch of paprika added to a recipe. To resign yourself to being the mere intermediary: that's true liberation. When your voice is the voice of the people, the author disappears (in any case no one wants to give up the royalties).

Apparently, there is a song that the Rolling Stones only play for themselves when they are doing sound checks or rehearsing. Written by Jagger and Richards, it's never been recorded. And they've taken every possible step to prevent anyone recording it in secret; it's said they only play it in the presence of their most trusted team members. No one else. Once or twice only, like a kind of mystical ritual before embarking on a tour. It's a melody that a few fortunate individuals are able to hum to themselves for a moment, until the band quickly imprints another song in its place, to ensure no one can retain it. The lyrics, or the lyrics as they're recollected, don't appear to make much sense. At some point, the band thought about recording it on a new album but, as good artists, they knew that its moment had passed. No one is eager to welcome a person raised from the dead or born after their time. Of course, the rumour has spread and people talk about other groups that have done the same, or they claim the story relates to a different band altogether. Beautiful melody, very simple harmonies, a devastating riff. Even better than 'Satisfaction', they insist – impossible. They've protected their treasure for forty years to save themselves from having to play it all the time.

Our best song hasn't been recorded yet, Keith Richards has said on more than one occasion, yet everyone wanted to see this as an artist's creative optimism. Jagger says the same thing from time to time, and once let slip a koan with a smile: *every now and again we play it.*

Sometimes when they're improvising, they'll play just a couple of chords. In videos, Jagger and Richards glance at each other and laugh.

It's said that someone made a recording during a

sound check in 1977 and it circulated in pirate copies. But no one's sure which of the hundred pirate ships it's on.

In reality, just like the secret formula for Coca-Cola, no one should care about knowing what it is. Since it went unheard at the time of its composition, the riff was never enfolded in the chrysalis of wonder that protects it from being merely obvious. Now it would just sound like any other track by the Rolling Stones.

Beethoven's Symphony No. 9 premiered in Vienna in 1824. The conductor had ordered the musicians not to pay attention to any indication given by the composer during the concert. He had already tried to conduct the rehearsal of his only opera, *Fidelio*, and it had been a veritable disaster. The players had finished, but Beethoven, with his eyes on the score, continued to move the baton; the contralto Caroline Unger had to tug on his sleeve for him to turn around and receive the applause of an exultant public, who had already interrupted the concert twice. The scene forms a delightful little caramel bonbon for any romantic spirit. Suffering, struggle and redemption form a perfect triangle: a geometry of pure art. Beethoven is a Moses who cannot enter the promised land. And there is something triumphal about the police ordering silence upon the fifth ovation, two more than protocol requires for the emperor, who is absent from the concert, perhaps because of the composer's republican ideology.

The deaf man's problem is that he can never stop hearing himself, like that thick, milky fog that prevents a blind person ever really getting the night back. But once his symphony sets out on its course, Beethoven attains true silence.

Before him, the void: the self-less zero where the children shout.

There are melodies that we never hear for the first time. What I mean is that we've been hearing them since before we learned to speak.

And since for a child everything is for the first time, the Ninth, the sand on the beach and a spinning top all pulse in the same way.

There is something of the mother's heartbeat in these melodies that have always been sounding.

Two rough waters merge when a baby hears a song.

The Atlantic and the Pacific meet in Drake Passage. There are terrible currents because the Pacific is higher – by just half a metre – than its sibling. Traversing the passage is far from easy: from the sailor's ear hangs the hoop that attests to the feat.

Below, the liquid child.

The first music always comes from the sky.

The mother's voice, an ocean empty of fish.

Without the assistance of the gramophone, how long did it take Brahms' 'Lullaby' to make its way around the world?

Like fairy tales, symphonies always have a happy ending.

Perhaps all the songs in the world have a happy ending.

A story with no baddies, that's what music sometimes seems like. Like the thought process of a galaxy.

And they lived happily ever after.

There's no sequel, the monster never returns.

Does a symphony, does any composition end because there's nothing more to tell? Because the tale is exhausted and anything else would be redundant?

Beethoven's Ninth ends on a light note, as if the musicians were hurrying to retire after having drawn back the curtain on something, fearful of receiving a ticking off. A secret brought to light, now lost forever.

Mahler concludes his Symphony No. 9 with a violin that moves away from the rest of the orchestra until it is left alone. The melody fades into the distance as if it were heading into the night.

Gradually slower and softer.

Towards peace and silence.

There is a truth in this journey because it's about a return.

So different to those bombastic finales that seem to go on forever, all fanfare and boom boom, almost like the mantra of someone who believes he has said everything there is to say.

Is this not how Mahler's Ninth should end, all pealing bells? After all, it is the final great symphony in a tradition begun by Beethoven.

But this doesn't happen, because his eldest daughter had died two years before.

And that violin is a lullaby that stretches out into the unsayable, and can only be heard from the aurora borealis.

That is why when the piece ends – it can be observed in countless videos – there is a silence that can last for up to three minutes. And the conductor continues to move the baton, because dead children too need to be rocked to sleep.

It seems that Mahler composed almost ninety minutes of music just to achieve that silence.

Claudio Abbado conducted the symphony in the Colón Theatre in Buenos Aires. A few days later Martín Kohan remarked: 'We only applauded because it is the custom. We shouldn't have made a sound. We should have left on tiptoe.'

If we watch videos of people born deaf at the moment they hear for the first time, it's impossible not to cry, or put a hand to our mouths. The people accompanying them – the doctors, family members – cannot help laughing. Something of the kind happens during childbirth.

The Who consummated their concert by destroying their instruments with genuine fury.

To end like this.

To end like this.

And to distinguish in this deafening noise not an end but the restless pulsing of a world that is being born.

And to remember forever that everything is possible when you stand on the shore, looking out to sea.

DA CAPO

In late 1956, the embassies of Russia and Canada resumed contact in order to pursue a policy of cultural exchanges. Of these, the one that had the greatest impact was Glenn Gould's visit to Russia in May the following year.

In a country that proclaims atheism to be the official state religion, an oeuvre like Bach's can only be treated with a great deal of suspicion. Under the conditions of the thaw, only his chamber music is to be played; no passions, cantatas or oratorios, not even whistled under the breath.

Gould lands in Moscow with fifty records of his *Goldberg Variations* and a book of Russian expressions under his arm. He has come to play six concerts, three in the capital and three in Leningrad. And since the two cities have always envied each other, tradition demands that neither accept uncritically what the other celebrates.

The pianist is not preceded by his reputation, which means that despite the cheap tickets, the Bolshoi Hall in the Moscow Conservatory is only one-third full. Nevertheless, just four counterpoints of *The Art of Fugue* suffice for the audience to head out into the street during the interval – and Russian intervals are as long as their novels – to telephone everyone they can reach. Enthusiastic telegrams speak of a Canadian fellow with an eccentric self-possession who plays the piano like no one else – and that is no trifle in a country full of musicians who play like no one else. And so, for the second half the hall is filled to the rafters, as they say, and many more are left outside. The following night chairs are added onstage, and over 900 people stand at the back to listen to the prodigy.

And perhaps because of its very eagerness to be different, exactly the same happened in Leningrad. The mirror image: a half-full theatre, the interval, crowds outside, chairs on the stage the second night, half an hour of applause.

But this time, they could shower him with blue flowers, because no one was at war any more.

The solar time difference between Toronto and Moscow is just under eight hours. Gould carries the day on his shoulders as he flies back to Canada, wearing it like an old coat. On landing, there's nowhere to hang the jacket.

The sunlight raking across the table in Scheherazade's tent.

After the concert where he performed the *Goldberg Variations* (a work that, the time has come to say, he never counted among his favourites), after dining and getting bored out of his skull because he despises both vodka and protocol, he tells the concierge he is not to be disturbed, lies down with the blankets up to his chin – he was always cold wherever he went – and his eyelids take barely the time of a haiku to fall shut. A few disordered thoughts before his perpetual insomnia disappears.

He father once recounted that as soon as little Glenn could sit up on his grandfather's lap, he didn't bang at the piano keys with his palms like all babies do, but fixated on just one key, pressing it down until the sound faded.

Over and over again.

Fascinated by the ever-fainter vibration.
Over and over again.
Insisting on what can only cease.
Over and over again.
Until reaching the moon.
Could there be a lovelier way to fall asleep?

Skopoynoy nochi.

CHARCO PRESS

Director & Editor: Carolina Orloff
Director: Samuel McDowell

www.charcopress.com

A special thank you to Annie McDermott who first edited
the translation of the chapter WARS for the publication of a
booklet previewing this title.

A Musical Offering was published on
90gsm Munken Premium Cream paper.

The text was designed using Bembo 11.5 and ITC Galliard.

Printed in September 2021 by TJ International
Padstow, Cornwall, PL28 8RW using responsibly sourced paper
and environmentally-friendly adhesive.

MIX
Paper from
responsible sources
FSC® C013056